I0576352

Immortal Spirit

An Ogre's Assistant Novel

By

D J Martin

For Karla.

Prologue

"You tell me you're older than Yoda. You must've seen some interesting stuff, huh?"

My familiar, a chocolate-brown cat named Fudge, interrupted his never-ending bath and looked at me.

"*It depends upon what you consider interesting. I have seen a lot in my time, yes.*"

"I'm not doing anything at the moment. Care to tell me about it?"

"*You want me to relate my life story? Why? Is not the fact that I have a lot of experience working with humans enough?*"

Fudge had spent enough time in my head to know that I always want to know about people. Not only am I a nosy person in general, I put people I meet in my stories. They've made my secret life as a paranormal romance author easy at times.

"Why not? Your story might give me some insight into the way you think and maybe then, I'd understand a little more about your role in my life."

Did I forget to mention? I'm a thirty-something single woman who just found out she's a witch. I'm what they call a late bloomer. It's inconvenient. And I just found out that the cat I thought was a pet is actually a familiar and that he's been rootling around in my head since he came to live with me. He knew about me. Turnabout is fair play, wouldn't you say?

"*You are not going to put me in one of your stories, are you?*"

"I'll be honest, I don't know. Maybe. But no one would recognize you anyway, so what are you worried about?"

My cat heaved a sigh. "*I know you well enough to know you will not stop asking. Refill my water dish, and I will tell you something of my life.*"

I grinned. As I performed the duty asked of me, I said, "Start at the beginning. First, how old are you, anyway?"

"I am not as old as some familiars but quite a bit older than many. In the way you humans count years, I am two thousand two hundred seventy-two years old and have been a familiar to eight magical beings before you.

"To understand my story, you need to have a basic understanding of familiars. Someone should have told you all this already but ...

"We are essentially present to help boost our human's power, although we also act as guardian and a repository for information. We have an elemental affinity, just as you do, and are assigned to a compatible witch or wizard. Familiar magic includes the ability to retain youthfulness in the body so we are able to stay with our human throughout their lifetime. As you have discovered, we can cause poison to our body to become inert and repair injury. There are exceptions, of course. A fatal blow such as a direct strike to the heart, lopping off the head, and the like will terminate the body. Should a witch or wizard allow that to happen, we do not return to them. They are charged with our safety, just as we are charged with theirs.

"When the witch or wizard dies, whether of natural causes or not, so does our corporeal body. Our spirit is then assigned to a different body by our ruling council. We always incarnate in a species appropriate as a companion for the magical person we are assigned to."

"How is a familiar made?" I interjected.

"We have not yet discovered the answer to that question. The Universe, in its infinite wisdom, decides when a spirit will be a familiar and when it will not. The oldest of our kind and head of our council, the Rottweiler you met, instinctively knows when a new spirit comes into being and adds it to the rolls kept by the Familiar Council.

"I will try to use terminology you are familiar with, but stop me if you do not understand something. I would prefer not to repeat myself."

"Before you continue, I have another question. I assume you didn't always live in the United States, so how many languages do you speak?"

"I do not know. In normal conversation, your mind interprets my thoughts as your native language, but I can also intentionally send words I learned from my other humans. As you learn other languages, I will add those words to my memory. Remember, part of a familiar's job is to act as a repository for information. So, may I continue?"

I poured myself a glass of wine, curled up in my chair and gave Fudge my full attention.

"I was born in the country you call Egypt in your year 252 BCE. My human was male. We were together for approximately two hundred fifty of your years. I then was assigned..."

I interrupted. "You sound like my college marketing professor, and he put me to sleep. I don't want a five-minute rote recitation of your life. I want to know about your humans, what you experienced with them, maybe even what *really* happened during some momentous times. Tell me a *story*!"

My cat sighed. "*Very well…*

Chapter One

As I said, I came into being in the year you currently number 252 BCE. This is the year I was born as a cat in what you call the country of Egypt. When I opened my eyes, my mother knew there was something different between me and my other siblings and pushed me out of her nest, as one would do the runt of the litter who was not expected to survive.

As the Universe had planned, a young man was nearby and took pity on my mewling. He took me home and hand-fed me until I was old enough to catch food on my own. Abou was a slave-assistant to a mage-priest overseeing part of the Library of Alexandria.

Abou had been purchased a few years earlier. He did not know his exact age, and his memories of his family are faint…they are overshadowed by a strong memory of hunger. About the only thing he remembered well is scrounging for food in the discards outside a tavern and being caught by a large man who turned him over to a slaver. It was a common enough occurrence in his town that no one came to look for him.

As a mage's assistant, Abou was taught how to make the various incenses that were burned at specific times of the day in the temple and to read and write, these last being necessary to know which scrolls or tablets to retrieve for the mage-priest's study. That allowed Abou to read the scrolls of knowledge from all parts of the known world housed in the part of the Library his master oversaw. He learned arithmetic to know how much his master was being charged for purchases and to keep a running account not only of the income and expenses from that particular part of the Library but also the master's personal accounts.

4

Familiars are born with the knowledge of our kind and the natural instincts of the species we occupy. Even as a newborn kitten, I knew what I was and what I was supposed to do. I must say, waiting for a corporeal body to grow to adulthood can be a frustrating experience.

Also frustrating, we cannot make ourselves known to our human until that person's magic manifests – usually around puberty but as you well know, it may be much later. It is not until then that their conscious mind will accept our presence. Abou's magic did not come in until two years after he found me. I spent those first two years being a simple cat. Once I had been weaned off the goat's milk Abou fed me, I killed rats alongside the other Library cats. They were my food but more importantly, by keeping my part of the Library rat-free, I helped preserve the papyrus scrolls and codices of knowledge.

When Abou reached puberty, his magic manifested in a most disheartening way. His master had accused him of mis-filing a scroll which, of course, he had not. "I did *not* put the scroll back," he cried. "Someone else must have, because I haven't touched that scroll in weeks!" At the same time, more than two dozen scrolls of precious knowledge flew from their holes in the shelves, three striking the mage-priest in the head. Thankfully, papyrus is much softer than a clay tablet and did no damage, either to the master or to the scrolls themselves.

The master looked about as the rolls of papyrus thudded to the floor and sighed. "You may not have touched *these* scrolls but you *will* put them back in their proper places!" Abou looked about wildly. How had the scrolls flown? What was happening? The master saw his confusion. "You have magic, boy, and it has just decided to show itself. I will teach you what you need to know. Now, put the scrolls back – in their proper places. I have things to do at the moment, but we will begin your magic lessons in the morning." The priest walked from the room and Abou, knowing of magic but not thinking *he* would have it, started cleaning up the mess he had inadvertently caused. His thoughts were scattered…he went from being amazed that *he* had magic to being scared of constantly causing problems such as making scrolls fly and possibly damaging them, to wondering what *more* his master would be teaching him and would that mean more hours of study?

I was finally able to fulfill my destiny as his familiar. My first few efforts had him running to his master for a headache remedy. After a lot of odd behavior on my part like nuzzling his face while he was practicing, Abou finally realized the pressure was me and that his magical efforts seemed more precise and stronger when he did not fight my help. My presence was accepted and we began our partnership. Telling him I wished for water in my dish was as easy as projecting a sense of thirst. Although I still killed rats when I found them in the Library, I mostly left that chore to the mundane cats. Abou quickly learned I preferred to share his meal of fish and was not averse to the occasional treat of goat's milk.

For some reason, he decided not to tell his master about me. Instead, the master thought me a favored pet and something of a security blanket. Abou took me with him nearly everywhere he went, including the market where he purchased supplies for his master. He even made a comfortable carrier for me when I let him know the sandy streets were too hot for my delicate paws in the summer and I disliked the mud in the rainy winter months.

I presume you studied something of that time in your history? No? Your educational system is sorely lacking. Then I must give you a brief history lesson before continuing.

Egypt was already an old country when I was born. They worshipped many gods, and magic was thought a gift of these gods. They did not know about the gene that transmits magical ability. It was a time when magic was a normal part of life, although the practice of it was limited to the priesthood. If a common person manifested magic, it was considered a sign that a male was destined for priesthood to a male god, a female as a priestess to a goddess, and those children were brought to a temple of the parents' choosing as an offering.

While Egypt was a country with many gods, there were some who were only worshipped locally and others who were considered state gods – or those whose worship was dictated by their ruler, or pharaoh. As with most civilizations, they tried to live peaceably with their neighbors, but if that could not be achieved, they made war. Egypt was at war quite a bit in my time there.

When Abou's magic manifested, his master took that as a sign from his god that Abou should follow in his footsteps as a mage-priest and began teaching Abou, rather than simply using him as an errand boy. When not helping visiting mages consult the ancient scrolls for a particular piece of knowledge, fulfilling his function as a priest to his god through ritual, and creating spells for petitioners, he taught Abou the Craft. I may have been there only to boost his power, but along with Abou, I learned the methods of human magic: how to manipulate energy, the herbcraft of the time and place, and their rituals to their gods. As an aside, camel grass, an ingredient in kyphi, one of their favorite incenses, makes me sneeze violently. Please do not ever use it.

"I have no idea what camel grass is, or kyphi for that matter. So I don't think you have to worry."

To continue. Abou's master was Water-affinity and did not know how to teach an Earth. He petitioned his gods to change Abou's element. Needless to say, the petition went unanswered. One cannot change their element! However, the master seemed to be attached to Abou, and rather than sell Abou to another mage-priest who was of the correct affinity, the master determined to make Abou the best priest he could. We were taught basic energy manipulation and what Water spells we could handle, but Abou and I were on our own to learn how to handle our element. That we accomplished by asking questions of other mages and practicing in our quarters at night.

Abou became proficient in all that was required of a priest, but his magic never seemed very strong, even when I added my own strength to his. Whatever he attempted, his master always seemed to accomplish with much less effort. In the beginning, I just thought the master was stronger.

One day Abou attempted to infuse a potion with simple healing energy and only managed a trickle of power, even with my help. The master brushed Abou aside and with no effort, I saw a good stream of energy make its way from his hands to the potion. I felt I had failed my human until I saw a glint in his master's eye then heard in my head, *"A familiar's magic is only as strong as his human's. In effect, you double his power. Your human is very weak, but only because his master siphons energy from him. You must help your human to break that cycle if he is to become all he may be."*

This was the first communication I had received from a superior since the welcome message I received when I was about six days of age. I sent a query back of, *"Why now?"*

And felt my head swing sideways as I received a metaphysical slap from what I perceived as a much larger paw. *"You have the knowledge within you, but it was obvious you needed a reminder. Be observant, youngling!"*

After another cuff on the ear, the presence withdrew from my mind. My head was reeling both from the slap and the realization that my superior was correct. I had seen the flows of energy between Abou and his master and ignored them. In my naiveté, I assumed humans knew to draw from the natural energy around them as I did … from the air, earth, water, even fire. Apparently, Abou's master did not adhere to this principle. Instead, he drew from his apprentice or anyone else who happened to be in proximity.

But how to tell Abou his master was an energy thief without dimming his adoration of the man who had pulled him from starvation and given him a purpose in life? How to tell him he must shield, when we only communicated in images and feelings?

That evening, back in our quarters, I interrupted Abou's study of a piece of papyrus by projecting a feeling of being wrapped, as they did their dead. Abou stopped reading and turned his attention to me.

"What are you trying to tell me, cat?" he asked.

I felt frustrated. If I could only tell him in the words he used as his master did! Then, it came to me. Abou did not like crowds and felt extremely uncomfortable whenever his master sent him to the bazaar to purchase materials. I projected that image and feeling to him, then once again, the mummy wrappings, followed by a feeling of ease.

Abou cocked his head. He did not understand. I heaved a sigh, hopped onto the table, and padded over to a pile of scrolls he had taken from the Library but not read. Some I did not know the subject matter, but others had to do with magic. *Those* I could sense to the point I had an idea of their content because when someone writes of magic, a little of it leaks into the ink and the material it is written on. I nosed one out of the pile I was fairly certain covered basic magical theory. Taking my clue, he pushed aside the one about water, unrolled the one I had indicated and started reading.

Halfway through, he turned to me with a smile on his face. "I finally understand. You're telling me I need to have a shield!"

As you know, cats do not smile, at least not in the human sense. To indicate approval, I purred and rubbed my face against his arm.

Abou absentmindedly petted me as he read further then pushed the scroll aside. He screwed up his face in concentration, and when nothing happened, said, "Where are you? I can't feel you. Why aren't you helping?"

I hung my head. While we can instruct on methods and construction, shielding is one of the few things a human must do on their own. I do not know why, but familiars cannot assist with this type of magic. I projected the image and feeling of being at a wall too high to jump.

Abou sighed. "I think I understand. You cannot help here. But you think this is important, so I will continue with my efforts."

It took some time but at last, a cocoon shimmered into existence around Abou. "I have it!" he exclaimed, and the cocoon disappeared.

That night the lamp almost ran out of oil as Abou read his papyrus, with me interrupting with a push to his mind each time his shield fell. The next night I did not have to interrupt as much and finally, after something over a week, he maintained his shield, even in his sleep.

The shield did not please the master, however. He made mention of it the first morning, yet could not argue with the reasoning that Abou hated crowds, felt a need for a shield, and needed to maintain it even in private so it became second nature.

Chapter Two

Over the following years, I noticed the master ageing and spending more time petitioning his god for youth, moving from one god to the next when his petition did not work. I privately laughed, as it appeared his gods had deserted him about the same time as Abou learned to shield. The flow of energy between the master and Abou had, naturally, stopped. I finally learned why he had kept Abou on even when the difference in element was discovered. He could draw from Abou but apparently few others.

Abou, on the other hand, flourished. He was a sponge for his master's teachings. After only ten years, he was his master's equal in magical ability – albeit in a different element – and had far outpaced him in knowledge of the Library. Patrons consulted Abou much more frequently than the master on where such-and-such a scroll or codex might be found, or where to look for particular information. My human was known far and wide for his specific knowledge of healing – both preparations and magical spells.

In my twenty-first year as a familiar, the master passed on. As a mage and priest, he was given a funeral second only to the Pharaoh's in pomp. All proper rites were observed, and after the requisite thirty days of mourning, Abou was considered a free man and officially took the master's place in the Library and temple.

Life was comfortable for the next two centuries, and nothing of import happened. Abou continued to shine in his position as a librarian, and his reputation as a mage grew, too. He was consulted by many, including the Pharaoh's advisors, on subjects ranging from military matters to healing potions. The Library held much information and Abou had ample opportunity to read most of it. He had a near-photographic memory and could recall almost everything he had read, making him a quicker reference than finding the appropriate subject matter in the Library.

My position as Abou's favorite pet was never questioned. Abou explained my unchanging presence by telling everyone that I was a descendant of "the original he had rescued so many years ago" and followed in his master's footsteps of attributing his own longevity to a gift from his gods. I understand the gods work in mysterious ways, so although he outlived several Pharaohs, his age was never questioned.

Our life was comfortable, that is, until the Romans came to Alexandria. As I understand it, political and military alliances are common among humans, and some Romans had allied themselves with powerful Egyptians. There were Roman ships docked in the harbor, and soldiers frequently roamed our streets. Many came to the Library to consult the papyri and codices for knowledge.

One night, several of their ships caught fire. The wind was blowing from just the right direction, and the fire spread to the part of the Library that Abou oversaw. We slept in rooms adjacent to our hall, and the smoke woke us.

Naturally, after something over two hundred years, Abou's magic came easily to him, and he was knowledgeable of all elemental work. He mustered up every ounce of energy we both could draw and called Water from the harbor in an effort to aid those already fighting the fire with buckets, as well a few Water mage-priests moving ocean water much more easily than we could. Although magicians were usually circumspect in their workings, Abou failed to look about him, and he was observed by a Roman soldier, who promptly hit Abou on the head with the hilt of his sword, knocking him out.

The soldier threw Abou over his shoulder like a sack of wheat and carried him to a ship that had been untouched by the fire. In the mêlée, I followed my human, unnoticed.

Abou was carried up a gangplank then down a set of steps into a large room below the main deck and deposited unceremoniously on the floor in front of a desk occupied by an older man. "He has magic," the soldier said, relating Abou's attempts to put out the fire.

"Excellent!" the man behind the desk said. "I could use a magician. See to it that he is made comfortable and any injuries are tended."

The soldier saluted, picked Abou up and carried him to another, much smaller room down a corridor where several other men were lying on cots, many with bandages over parts of their bodies. The soldier put Abou on a cot, told the man in charge he was to be made comfortable by order of the trierarch, then left. I curled up under his cot, determined to find out what our new life would be like.

Abou woke about an hour later, and the man in charge, a physician I gathered, asked him in halting Egyptian if he spoke the Roman language, to which Abou replied in the same halting voice, "Read, yes. Speak a little." Abou had had enough contact with them to pick up a few words and phrases.

"My head hurts. Where am I and why have I been taken?" Abou continued in his native language.

In Egyptian, the physician continued, "Hit on head. Commander needs help. You there. Now here. I put cloth on head to help."

From underneath the cot, I projected enough images to Abou so he would know exactly what had happened to him. Once understanding the headache, Abou questioned the physician about the poultice on his head. Through words in both languages and gestures, he learned that it was an herb found in mountains that the Greeks had discovered healed bruises.

"You healer?" inquired the physician.

"No, scribe." Abou replied. "Like knowledge."

"Ah. Explains trierarch's interest. He like knowledge, too."

The physician turned to another patient, and the older man I had seen earlier walked into the room. After inquiring as to his men (some would live, others it was doubtful), he asked if Abou was able to leave the treatment room.

"Yes. He has a bump on his head and a headache but otherwise will be fine."

The older man gestured to Abou to follow him. We did. In silence.

Back in the older man's quarters, he indicated that Abou should sit and finally noticed me. In perfect Egyptian, he said, "I am told you are a magician. You may serve me in such a capacity or be a slave and help row this ship. Your cat is welcome here – we have too many rats."

Abou had never done much physical labor and truthfully, had retained his scrawny build. Rowing would probably have killed him, and he knew it. However, he also knew something of Roman life.

"How would I serve you? Magic is forbidden in your culture. Perhaps dying as a slave would be preferable to dying as a magician."

"I am Greek. My culture accepts magic. I and my ship serve Rome. In their culture, magic is technically forbidden, but only black magic is prosecuted. My soldier tells me you can call water. As *trierarch* or captain of a ship, being able to manipulate my ship through water with ease would earn me great rewards if I can get goods to ports more quickly and safely than my competitors. I assume you have other skills I could put to use, as well."

Abou was nothing if not truthful. "Although I can work with Water, it is not my true element, and I am not strong in it. I will do my best to help where I can but I may not be able to do everything you ask."

The captain thought for a moment. "I will take every edge I can get. If you can call water from the harbor all the way to the Library, you should be able to do whatever it is I will require. I will keep you."

So, their partnership began. Technically, as a captured barbarian, Abou was a slave. Practically speaking, the captain had just garnered himself a *tabularius* and *librarius*. Abou became the official keeper of financial records and scribe. Secretly, Abou was the captain's mage...helping the seas move the ship where he could without using so much energy he fainted; easing the burden of the rowing slaves which kept them in better health; surreptitiously helping the *medicus* treat injuries to some of the *trierarch*'s favored sailors with healing spells; causing difficulties aboard an enemy ship; and basically making himself useful wherever the captain deemed he could be of use. Abou also learned to speak the Greek and Roman languages and after a time, could switch between the three with ease.

I was put to use, as well, but not always helping Abou. Rats were common aboard ships. Although all the food was stored in clay jars with stoppers, grain spillage was common, and the vermin feasted on it. I ate well and the cook gave me treats of fish to reward my efforts. As long as I literally stayed out from underfoot, no one on the ship bothered me, and if I needed to be at Abou's side for some reason, it was simple enough to walk with a dead rat in my mouth to where I needed to be. These I spat overboard as soon as I could if I did not need to eat them for sustenance. I had become accustomed to a better diet and ate rats as rarely as possible.

Our quarters were better than most of the slaves on the ship. Abou slept on a pallet in the captain's quarters with me curled beside him. At first, the captain had him sleep right in front of the door, but when he discovered Abou's lack of fighting skills, our pallet was moved to a far corner. It was not as comfortable as our bed in the Library but could have been far worse.

For five years, we did not set foot on dry land. Even when the ship was in port to take on supplies or offload cargo, Abou was not given shore leave with the freeman crew, but locked away with the rest of the slaves. The captain did not want him running away, although I was not sure where we would go – we sailed throughout the Mediterranean but never saw Alexandria again.

Finally, the captain decided he had earned enough to retire. Rather than going back to his native Greece, he purchased a house near Tharros, Sardinia, which allowed him a view of his beloved sea. He kept Abou, the ship's cook, and several other slaves, and sold both the ship and the rest of the crew to another Greek captain who also wanted to earn his rewards working for the Romans.

The captain brought his wife, three daughters-in-law, and several grandchildren from Greece to the house in Tharros. His sons, also ship captains, visited when they were able. It was a crowded household, and the grandchildren had the strange idea that I was nothing more than a pet. I would be snatched from my spot near Abou's workbench to be cuddled and petted at a moment's notice. It was enjoyable to a certain extent but quickly became tiresome, although for Abou's sake I never clawed or bit when I wanted them to stop. I simply wriggled out of their grasp and scampered to a place they could not reach. I was glad when the children grew and I was no longer a plaything.

Abou had read enough in the Library and spoken with enough Romans in our five years aboard ship to learn the Roman ways of magic. Although he was known as the captain's scribe, his reputation as a mage rapidly spread. Neighbors and friends of the captain and his household would ask permission to consult on various personal matters.

He had learned to be flexible in his workings: he gave inscribed lead sheets to the captain's Roman friends, amulets to the Greeks, various incense mixtures to all. After years of working mostly health, fair winds, and money spells, he added legal matters, love, and even race-fixing to his repertoire. I found the human needs interesting.

Abou added to the captain's coffers even on dry land, so except for the collar denoting him as a slave, Abou had a life almost as comfortable as the captain's. We had our own room in the house rather than sharing accommodations with the other slaves; Abou ate the same rich food as was prepared for the family; and he was free to decide which requests for magical assistance he would take on and what the captain would receive for his services.

The captain was not a young man when he had taken Abou aboard ship, and nothing was going to halt the ravages of age, inactivity, and overindulgence on a human body. Abou tried his best to assist the physician in his efforts to save the captain after a massive heart attack, to no avail. Unfortunately, those efforts were also the downfall of Abou. Not a young man himself and despite my warnings, Abou drew too much energy into his body in an effort to save his master. His heart stopped moments after the captain was declared dead, and I found myself in the ether.

Chapter Three

For your edification, the ether is like being in thick, gray smoke. Your spirit would be lost forever, but familiars always know where we are, even if we cannot actually see anything. From somewhere, I heard a deep voice say, *"You have done well, youngling, although you have much to learn. There are ways to block your human from drawing too much energy."*

Images crowded my head on ways to block parts of the brain to prevent a human from causing harm to him or herself. *"Remember what I have shown you. Your human was old so it is no great loss, but that may not always be the case. Protecting your human from himself is part of the reason for your existence."*

I felt a push from behind, and the next I knew, I was chipping my way out of an egg, surrounded by others doing the same with their beaks. The next few weeks saw me in a stick-lined nest built into the rafters of an old, decaying manmade building where no man came, eating worms and insects from the beaks of my mother and father.

My siblings and I were just learning to fly when one day a strong storm ravaged our area. Two men, one older, one younger took shelter in our building. My parents both sat on the nest, attempting to keep us safe, but the nest was blown from its perch and we all tumbled out. I landed right in the lap of the child. I could not see where the rest of my family went, but I knew I was where I was supposed to be.

"It is a sign, Korbis," said the older man. "You must care for the bird."

The boy cradled me in his arms as he slept, and when the next day dawned bright and sunny, attempted to perch me on his shoulder as they walked. Not yet well able to manage my balance, I promptly fell off and fluttered around in an effort to fly back up to my designated perch. After several attempts, I finally managed the four-foot flight. Korbis cooed at me and stroked my feathers, then winced as I dug my talons into his shoulder in an effort to stay put.

As they walked, the older man taught my new human about me.

"Your bird is a chough. Black birds have many associations in many cultures and most of them, including ours and that of our overlords, are lucky ones. Therefore, you must protect your bird from others, as they might try to steal it for good luck of their own.

"You must encourage his efforts to fly so he can get his own food. He will eat almost anything, although grasshoppers seem to be a favorite food for adults. In the meantime, we will try to find an ant colony when we stop."

They did indeed make camp in a grassy area with enough ants for me to make a full meal. Most of these I caught by hopping around, but I also managed a flight of a few yards to spot another anthill. After they had eaten their meal of bread and dried fruit washed down by some watered wine, the older man took a piece of leather from his pack, and with a length of sinew and a bone needle, sewed it to the shoulder of Korbis' tunic. "This will prevent his claws from digging any more holes into your skin. We will need to find a thicker piece of leather when he gets a little older because he'll go right through this one with his talons."

About noon the next day, we came to a large field of grapevines. After inquiring of one of the workers tending the vines, we made our way some distance farther and up a small hill to a compound. After speaking with the steward answering the door, the older man presented himself to the lord of the manor. "I believe you are expecting me. My name is Orison, and I am your new vintner."

"Yes, yes, man. I am grateful you were able to take the position. The sons of my previous vintner are yet too young to know the job. I assume this is your son?"

"No, sir. He is my nephew, the son of my dead sister. He is also my apprentice and is learning my trade. While he learns, he also helps tend vines."

"You are both welcome. I presume that is some sort of pet bird? We have a dovecote where it can stay. My steward will show you that on the way to your quarters. As you undoubtedly saw on your way here, the vines are just blossoming. Until they are ready for pressing, I would like you to inspect our cellar, consult with my physician on which spices to use for his needs, and get to know the people and routine around here. I must leave for a week or so, but I will speak with you on my return."

I was unceremoniously left in a room covered in droppings with a bunch of stupid doves. This was not where I wanted to be! However, some time later, Korbis came to get me.

"I'm sorry," he said while holding out his arm, indicating I should perch there. "I had to leave you here when the steward was watching. I also had to see what our quarters were like. We have a window, and Orison has fashioned a perch for you next to it." He stroked my back as he walked down the tower stairs and finally into a room at the end of a long hallway. It smelled of wine and herbs.

Korbis put me on my perch, and I watched while he and Orison unpacked their belongings. They were just finishing when a man came into the room.

"Orison! I heard the new vintner had the same name as my old friend and just had to see. When did you develop that skill? And who's the youngster?"

Orison and the older man clasped arms. "Tal! Are you the physician here? Tell me it's so. The young man is my apprentice. I am passing him off as my nephew. How have you been?"

While Korbis finished putting their meager belongings away, the two older men opened a bottle of wine found in a cupboard, mixed it with water in a pitcher and, sitting at the table in the room, caught up. I eavesdropped and found out that both older men practiced magic and had been taught by the same master. Korbis was the orphaned son of a healer Orison had had an affair with, and Orison had learned the job of vintner from another mage he had encountered on his travels.

"Honestly, Tal, being a vintner is no difficult thing once you know your grapes. It's just a question of when to harvest which varietal, which to blend with other varietals, which go well with herbs for your use … it's fairly easy, pays well, and gives me quite a bit of free time to do – other things."

"It's easy being a physician here, as well. There's good air, not a lot of fighting, and few accidents. Mostly I treat the illnesses of the local children, with a few broken bones thrown in for good measure and gather herbs in season. The previous vintner, may the gods protect him on his journey, knew nothing of herbcraft, so I also oversaw the making of medicinal wines. Are you up on the local plants?"

Korbis got bored and decided to go exploring. I fluttered my way to his shoulder, and we went outside through the door opposite the one to the hallway.

We found ourselves outside the manor and looking down the hill at the rows upon rows of grapevines. "There's plenty of room for you to fly around, and I'll wager a lot of bugs, too." Korbis pulled me off his shoulder and threw me up into the air. I was growing stronger and managed a brief flight before I saw a snack – a juicy looking grasshopper on the edge of the grape fields. Two more and I was full for the moment, so flew back to Korbis, who was wandering around, looking at the compound itself and eying the fields where not only men but several women were tying vines to supports and checking the vines' health.

We were called back to the room by Orison. "We dine with the other workers in the common hall, but you must leave your bird here. We will look at the window tomorrow in full light to see how it can be adapted for his use while still keeping out the weather."

The next morning, Orison and Tal together refashioned the leather latch on the wooden shutter so I could open it myself. Although Orison knew what I was, he explained to young Korbis that choughs are exceptionally intelligent birds, which was why it only took a few tries for me to master it. I now had the freedom to go find my own food whenever I was hungry.

Orison and Korbis spent a lot of time in the fields, getting to know not only the workers but the grapes. I finally learned to fly long distances and between flights, kept many an insect from invading the fields.

Spring turned to summer, which slowly turned to fall and the first harvest overseen by Orison. Everyone was busy picking, pressing, or catching the juice in clay amphorae, which were taken into the cellar for fermentation. Orison oversaw the pressing, noting which was free-running juice (the best and once fermented, sold to the Romans for a hefty sum), first-press (for the lord's table, the medicinal wines, and also used to pay Roman taxes) and second-press (for the household). Korbis, by the marks made by Orison on the amphorae, directed the storage in the cellar.

During this first harvest, Korbis hit puberty, which means his magic manifested. Thankfully, it was in our room in the evening, so no one but Orison saw the piece of rock fly out of the fireplace when Korbis lost his temper in regard to keeping company with one of the lord's daughters.

"Ah, your magic has finally manifested," Orison said as he calmly picked up the rock and replaced it in the fireplace, waving his hands to firmly affix it to its neighbors.

"I...what?" Korbis sputtered.

"You knew your mother had magic, yes?" Korbis nodded.

"You knew what she did out of sight of curious eyes was to be kept secret?" Korbis nodded yet again.

"Your mother entrusted you to me on her deathbed not just because I could teach you a trade, but because she knew your magic would come in when you hit puberty and I could teach you about that, as well.

"You have a lot to learn. We will now commence lessons in the evenings – and during the day in the winter months. In the meantime, you must keep control of your temper, especially when we're not alone. Bird, I know you hate enclosed spaces, but you'll have to stay in the cellar with him while he works. I'm counting on you to control him if he can't control himself."

Korbis looked from Orison to me and back again. "Huh?"

"Your bird is your familiar. He'll help you with your magic. You'll get to know him better during your lessons. Now, it's bedtime. It's going to be another long day tomorrow."

When Korbis had bedded down, I introduced myself in his mind. That caused him to sit straight up in bed, yelling for Orison, who quickly relit the lamp.

"What is it, boy?"

"There are spirits here! I felt one!"

Orison laughed, which caused Korbis to become angry. When he opened his mouth to yell, I quickly dampened his anger and projected an image of myself along with the calming energy. Korbis continued to hold his mouth open while looking first at me then at Orison.

"There probably are spirits here, but I do not think they're bothering with a young boy. Did you feel pressure in your head, sort of like the start of a headache but not quite?"

Korbis closed his mouth long enough to swallow, then nodded and said, "Yes, and now I can't get the picture of my bird out of my head. I was mad, and now I feel just fine. What is happening to me?"

Orison laughed again. "Remember what I said about your bird being your familiar? I believe he is introducing himself while at the same time, controlling your temper so you don't cause the entire house to collapse with your unwarranted anger."

"How do you know this?" Korbis asked.

A note of sadness touched Orison's voice. "I once had a familiar, as well. Sadly, he was killed by hunters some time ago, so I am left alone. But I do remember our days together. Guard your bird well, Korbis, and treasure him."

Orison extinguished the lamp, and I let go of the block on Korbis' emotions. I projected an image of Korbis asleep on his bed then a second one of me asleep on my perch. He got the message and shortly, his conscious mind drifted off and he started dreaming of spending time amongst the vines with the lord's daughter. This did not concern me, so I disassociated myself with his mind and I, too, went to sleep.

"You mean you can see **everything** *in my head, even my dreams?"*

Yes, of course. If you will recall, I have seen your dreams in the past and was able to tell you when they were true dreams. As I have also told you, most of it does not interest me so I, as you say, tune it out. May I continue?

Korbis was like you, a fast learner. Within three years, he had outpaced Orison in power. However, he had almost no interest in learning the vintner's trade. Instead, with the lord's permission, he became apprenticed to the lord's physician, Tal.

This is where Korbis shone. He learned from Tal which herbs were used for what, how to blend them to make medicinal wine, how to use mechanical methods as well as magic to set a broken bone…all the tools of a physician of the time. Several times a year, a legion or more of the Roman army passed through the area, and both Tal and Korbis assisted their *medicos*, learning from one another, although Tal and Korbis were careful to hide their magical nature. The Romans did not take kindly to magic unless it was in the form of a rite to a god or goddess. A Roman god or goddess, I might add. The gods worshipped by the locals were not the same, although the more the Romans settled in the area, the more their religion was adopted.

By the time Korbis was in his late twenties, Tal was encouraging him to find a girl, get married and start raising a family. Little did anyone know that my human had retained his first crush on the lord's daughter, Munika, who had been married off to the son of an adjoining landowner when she was sixteen. Her husband had joined the Roman army, been killed in a battle somewhere and she had returned to her parents' home a childless widow. The problem was, she was not a witch, and like most people, Korbis did not want to far outlive his spouse. Tal was able to ferret this piece of information out of Korbis, and they had a discussion about it.

"Love does not distinguish between magical and non-magical people, Korbis," Tal told him. "Munika is now a widow, meaning she will not be considered a prime catch. The lord has already provided one dowry, and I doubt he will provide another, making her even less desirable. You, on the other hand, are a free man, have a verifiable skill, can provide for her even if you live elsewhere, and aren't too bad looking in the bargain. Does she share your feelings?"

Korbis nodded, miserable in his predicament. "Yes, but she does not know of my magic. I have been afraid to tell her. She learned Roman ways during her marriage and now speaks against it."

"Ah," Tal said in understanding. "Yet you still love her."

"Yes!" Korbis cried. "She is beautiful, sweet, gentle, everything a man could wish for."

"In that case, there is a spell that can be used to make you appear to age. Mind you, it won't be as quickly as a human will age, and you will get all the aches and pains associated with advancing years but if you can hide everything else, this will make you appear human."

At this, I cautioned my human, and it was not easy to do since I had not yet developed mind-speech. The spell works, yes. But it can come with complications.

"Such as…?"

Think on it, my human – Amy. If they had children, how would he explain his great longevity to them after his wife died? How would he explain it to his adult grandchildren or even great-grandchildren? Worse yet, what if he did not maintain the spell and started to appear younger? And if a descendant should exhibit magical abilities, and it is likely one or more would, what then?

You will recall the wizard, Gregory, I believe he is called, encountered difficulty with his non-magical father when his magic manifested. He was just forced to leave his home. In the Roman culture, it could mean a death sentence.

Korbis was better off with a local girl who had not been corrupted by Roman influence. The locals were what you term Celtiberians who still accepted magic in all its forms, although they preferred that its practice was not done openly to prevent retribution by the ever-growing Roman presence.

Once Korbis thought about all I had cautioned, although he was extremely unhappy, he saw the logic.

"I don't want to be deceitful," he told Tal. "I also can't stay here and watch her marry someone else."

Tal inclined his head knowingly. "I was just thinking that I'd been here thirty years and it was time for me to be moving on. I would be delighted to have you as a traveling companion. However, if we both are leaving, we will have to wait until the lord finds another physician. Can you tolerate your situation until then?"

Korbis nodded glumly. "I will have to, won't I? I also need to tell Munika I am leaving with you. She will not be understanding."

And so, Tal gave the news to the lord, who seemed to take it in stride. Korbis told Munika that he was leaving with Tal. That did not go so well. Naturally, Munika did not understand why Korbis was leaving her and as with most women, tears of sadness then anger flowed. Her rage served Korbis well, though, as she went out of her way to avoid seeing him. That made the break-up easier to bear.

In less than a month, an older Roman *medico* was persuaded to take up residence, and we were on our way. Tal did not wish to meet up with any Romans (who may have conscripted them) so we made our way through the countryside rather than use the wide thoroughfares constructed by the occupying army.

Chapter Four

For over forty years, Tal and Korbis traveled the province of Aragon, settling for about ten years in any one place before Tal got the itch to move on once again. At each town, Tal would start a garden with seeds he had saved of the healing herbs he knew best: thyme, rosemary, parsley, mint, lavender, and lemon balm. This garden announced to the neighbors that a healer was amongst them, and the two wizards did not lack for business.

Although the Roman influence was felt nearly everywhere, they always settled in towns where the locals only tolerated Roman rule. In this way, they knew their services would not only be wanted, but no one would report them for the practice of witchcraft. But one early fall day, Tal made a fatal mistake...

It was grape harvest season, and there was always work to be found for a physician during this time, treating various ailments and injuries of the vine workers. He and Korbis were passing through the city of Caesaraugusta, which lay in the valley of the Ebro River – a prime area for wine grapes.

At that time, the Romans were spiritually divided: some held faith with the old gods while others were following the new Christ. In the city of Caesaraugusta, a temple to Diana had been taken over and was being re-consecrated as a Christian church. Tal and Korbis happened to pass in front of the building on their way to find lodgings for the night when a fight broke out between the arguing factions.

Whenever Romans fought, injuries followed, and within minutes, the two men were caught up in the mêlée, attempting to help those who had fallen. As I perched on the roof of the temple, Korbis helped a woman who had been hit on the head to the steps of the building. Digging in his pouch, he gave her a handful of arnica flowers he had obtained in trade, telling her to use them in a poultice on the lump that was forming on her forehead.

Down in the street, one man was bleeding out from a stab wound to his side. Tal knew he would have to act fast to save the man's life, so in addition to ripping off a part of his robe to staunch the blood flow, he injected some healing magic into the man to start the process of knitting together the blood vessels.

A bystander saw the blood stop pouring out of the man, and started yelling, "Magic! He's a magician! Guards! Magic!"

That effectively stopped the fight, as everyone turned to look at Tal. Neither side had much use for magic, so it did not take long for them to turn on a common enemy. In the blink of an eye, two men who had been guarding the church were hauling Tal up off the man he had been trying to save. Korbis heard the shouting and began to make his way through the crowd to Tal.

"Run, boy! Save your own life," Tal shouted with his head hung, to avoid laying suspicion on Korbis.

Korbis froze in his spot. Although they had frequently discussed the possibility of death due to the changing customs, he was indecisive as to whether to abandon his friend and mentor. I had no choice but to project an image of Korbis being beheaded, which would have happened had he stayed. Whether Korbis exhibited any signs of magic or not, he would have been guilty by association.

With a last look back at Tal held fast in the burly arms of the two soldiers, I took flight and Korbis turned away from Tal, walking as calmly as he could away from the fracas in front of the temple.

That night within the confines of his room at an inn on the edge of the city, Korbis mourned his friend. Tal was a jovial man, always ready with a joke, which eased the minds of many of the patients he tended. He also helped Korbis with his magic which, in turn, strengthened my connection to my human.

Korbis vowed to leave the Roman-occupied area, but where to go? He had learned from talking to people over the years that the Roman influence was widespread. However, he had heard there was an island far to the north where they had little, if no influence. The first step, then, was to make our way to the coast and hope to find a trading ship to take us to that mysterious place.

We left Caesaraugusta the next morning. Korbis did not know where he wanted to go – only that it needed to be toward a major port. We followed the Ebro eastward, reasoning that where it flowed into the ocean would be as good a place as any to look for a ship. As we had in our travels with Tal, Korbis plied his trade as a traveling physician, staying first at this farmhouse, then that townhouse, trading his healing skills for lodging, food, and the occasional coin.

During this time, Korbis kept his magical skills under wraps. Walking the Roman-built roads, we saw far too many soldiers and citizens dressed in the Roman style to be comfortable. In those places where he felt relatively safe, he would cast a quiet charm for a young lady to find love, or for a young couple to have a good harvest, bringing in a little extra money to aid them in starting their life together.

Two years later, we smelled brackish air – we had reached the delta. Inquiring of a traveler met coming in the opposite direction, Korbis learned there was a small port just a day's journey farther. We camped that night in the open and the next day arrived at the Roman trading post that doubled as a port.

How different the ocean air than that next to a river! I found it heavier and had to adjust my flight to compensate. Then there was the salt that accumulated on my feathers! I was not meant to live in such an environment and told Korbis so by projecting images of the Ebro valley we had left.

My needs, however, did not factor into his decision. Korbis wandered the area next to the docks, discreetly inquiring of this mystical northern island where the Romans did not hold sway. Although more than a few eyebrows were raised, no one turned him in, nor was information forthcoming until late in the day. When he stopped for food and a glass of wine, he met an old, grizzled sailor who said we might have better luck in a larger port.

"Not much happens here," he told Korbis. "You'd be better off asking about faraway places where more ships put in."

"Where would you suggest I go?" Korbis asked him.

"I understand there are learned men at Neapolis who might be able to point you in the right direction. It's a large port with a lot of rich people. There must be someone there who knows which island you're speaking of."

"And how would I get to this Neapolis? I'm only a simple physician without much to pay for passage."

"As it happens, we ply the Mare Nostrum and Neapolis is the other end of our journey. However, our captain has the flux in a bad way. That's why I and my fellows are here, rather than on board, making ready to set sail. We're a small ship without our own physician, so if you can help the captain, he may see fit to carry you on our next voyage. Then again, he may not."

Having nothing to lose, Korbis asked the man to show him to his captain.

Within the confines of the captain's cabin, the odor was bad even for me. I cannot imagine how the humans stood it. The captain was lying in his bunk, curled in the fetal position with his arms pressed against his abdomen. Next to the bunk was a slop pail – this is where the smell was coming from. I flew back out on deck and listened to Korbis' mind as I perched on one of the masts.

Korbis determined that the man had eaten some bad food. Or possibly been poisoned. But he guessed it was tainted food. That, he knew, would pass on its own in a couple of days. Telling the hovering sailor that he needed a jug of watered wine, he told the captain he would prepare a medicine that should help him in a few hours.

The sailor returned with a cup of watered wine. Into this, Korbis crumbled some berry leaves from his pouch and held the cup over the flame of the candle on the captain's desk to heat it.

Once he was satisfied with the medicated wine, he helped the captain to sit and fed the wine to him in sips.

Once again, the hovering sailor was pressed into service as a cabin boy. Broth was needed, as was bread. The ship apparently did have a cook, so it did not take long for the required food to appear. Although Korbis had to cajole him, the food was consumed, and the captain finally fell into a slumber.

(This entire sequence took far longer than I have described, as the captain attempted to empty his bowels several times. I do not think I need to describe that in detail.)

"I have done what I could," Korbis told the sailor. "He should start feeling better by the morning. May I stay to ensure that he does?"

"Not my ship, but as my son is in no position to gainsay me, I will invite you to stay in his cabin in case he should need you."

"Your son, you say?" Korbis was surprised.

"Aye. I had no desire to a captaincy, but he wanted the money that comes with it. I prefer less responsibility."

Korbis told the truth. The captain was feeling somewhat better by morning. Another dose of herbs in wine and more broth and bread had him on deck by noon. Physically pale and weak, the captain nonetheless gave orders to make the ship ready to sail with that afternoon's tide. Korbis was granted passage to Neapolis in payment for his services and his "pet bird" was welcomed as a means for keeping seagulls from eating the fish caught daily for food. I may have been somewhat smaller than a seagull and my beak not nearly as long, but I was quicker and able to maneuver better in flight to chase those garbage hounds away.

Our trip was, as you say, smooth sailing. The ship skimmed along the water, even after leaving a port on the northern end of Sardinia, when it had to zig-zag to travel in a more southerly direction.

However, as I had pointed out earlier to Korbis, I was a *land* bird. The captain kept a clean ship, and there was little in the way of bugs for me to eat. Korbis kept me alive by feeding me offal from the fish caught for the sailors' food, but my digestive system was not happy. Thankfully, we were only at sea five days. Longer, and I may not have lived.

After taking his leave of the captain, Korbis wandered the streets of Neapolis with his jaw hanging in awe. We had never seen such a large city, much less one as cosmopolitan. Greeks in chitons and Romans in togas walked side-by-side along the thoroughfares with no signs of animosity.

At the entrance to a Roman bath, Korbis asked a man if there was a place a physician could ply his trade. Taking one look at the obvious barbarian in his breeches, tunic and cloak, the man grabbed Korbis by the arm and dragged him up one street and down another. I had taken flight to find *real* food (which was plentiful) but at a feeling of alarm from Korbis, I returned and followed them to a large house on a hill. Korbis was hauled through the doorway. I settled on the branch of a fig tree in the courtyard to await further happenings.

"You are a physician, you say. Heal my daughter."

Through Korbis' mind, I saw a pale young lady lying on a bed. Were it not for the shallow rise and fall of her breast, I would have thought her dead. The room was as lavish as the corridors Korbis had been dragged through: frescoes on the walls, carved furniture, *and* a shrine to Athena in the corner. Although the man spoke fluent Latin, they were Greek. That was fortunate.

Korbis asked a few questions, got fewer answers and, heaving a sigh, used his magic to look at her. A tumor on her brain told him why she did not wake. He relayed his findings to the father.

"Magos, you will heal her. Or I will turn you in to the Roman *tribunus* who is visiting his father, the senator, next door."

I flew through the open window to perch on Korbis' shoulder. The father did not even bat an eye. Not stopping to wonder how the man knew he had magic, Korbis nodded and proceeded to draw energy from the environment *and* that which I fed to him. More than an hour later, he had carefully evaporated the tumor. The girl's breathing deepened, and color started returning to her cheeks. This was in stark contrast to Korbis' drawn appearance and my desire to do nothing but eat a full meal and sleep for two days. It had been a difficult "operation." Even in those days, it was known that any medical condition affecting the brain could have disastrous effects.

Korbis was fed and given a room, not quite as lavish, in which to lay his head. We both slept for the better part of a day. When we woke, a man guarding the door gestured, and Korbis followed him to a salon where our host and several others reclined on couches.

Korbis was formally introduced to his host, Kalchas, a wealthy factory owner. The conversation reverted to Greek and I translated the tale Kalchas was telling as best I could with images. I am not certain if Korbis understood what I was trying to tell him. Switching to Latin, Kalchas informed Korbis that he was now a member of his household. He was not to leave the house unless given express permission to do so. His duties would include seeing to the health of the household, instructing the gardeners which herbs he required to be planted and harvested, and assisting Kalchas' friends when asked to do so.

Slavery! Gilded, but a cage, nonetheless. Korbis was dismayed – he would never find his mysterious island. I, on the other hand, while disappointed for my human, was happy I would not have to travel the seas again.

Life settled into a routine. Korbis became accustomed to wearing a chiton rather than breeches (he complained frequently of the breeze on his nether regions), learned to speak passable Greek and, with a large herb garden, cured the ailments of the household and those of Kalchas' friends. And like his predecessor, Abou, he prepared love charms, amulets for legal cases, and talismans for race- or fight-fixing. The young lady he had healed, Agathe, never the sharpest knife in the drawer, was married off to that *tribunus* within three months. That afforded Kalchas an entrée into even higher Roman society.

A little over a year into our captivity, Kalchas decided to retire. He turned over the operation of his factory to his oldest son, and management of his distribution network to the middle son. The oldest son got the house in Neapolis and, much to my dismay, we moved to a smaller house in the beautiful seaside city of Herculaneum with its salt air. It was just a few leagues away so Kalchas could still keep an eye on his children.

Here, Korbis had to be even more circumspect. Herculaneum was at that time more Roman than Greek, although the Greeks had founded the city. Kalchas devoted the majority of his time to his new-found love of Roman politics. He and the senator (who had also retired and relocated) would spend hours discussing and debating what was happening in Rome. Korbis spent a good deal of time treating the gout so prevalent in the older, less active generation that was Kalchas and his friends.

Then, one fateful late summer day, the mountain Vesuvius started billowing ash. No one, not even the oldest alive, remembered that it was a volcano. At the first signs, panic hit the city, and everyone rushed to the sea, hoping to take a boat far away. Korbis and several other slaves were told to pack Kalchas' valuables and join him at a specific spot along the shoreline. I was told to follow the master so Korbis could be sure of meeting him in the correct place. I took flight, but we never made it. The last thing I remember of that life is air hotter than an oven.

Chapter Five

I was in the ether for what seemed an inordinate length of time. As I had no human, I had no reference points of time and place to leave on my own. When I inquired, I was told, "*Patience, youngling.*" I later discovered that not only are we paired with a human based on our elemental affinity, the Council also matches personalities. Apparently, there was no human to match me with for that period of time. Thinking back on my humans, I am not certain what that says about me, but no matter. I opened my eyes to find a teat in my mouth – I was nursing. A quick glance around told me I probably was a dog and had five siblings. The sound of small children squealing, laughing, playing, whatever small children do, assaulted my ears.

As soon as I'd released the nipple I was sucking on, small hands picked me up, and I was crushed against a chest. "This one is mine," a voice chirped.

"You'll have to speak with your Da about that," an older, female voice said. "You know he plans on selling them."

The little voice whined, "But Aedan has his own dog. I want one!"

"Aedan uses his for hunting. Girls don't hunt. What would you do with your own dog?"

The human crushing me against her chest thought for a moment. "Girls do too hunt. Brigid goes with the men. I've seen her. I can hunt, too!"

The older voice sighed. "As I said, you'll have to ask your Da. Now put him back with his mother."

I was replaced back with my siblings, and after some arguing, secured a spot right next to my mother and fell asleep.

As you might imagine, the little girl got her way. Aoife was appropriately named after the greatest Irish female warrior. She had no compunction about fighting, even with her fists, to get what she wanted. Her older brothers laughed at her attempts to beat them to a pulp; younger siblings did their best to stay out of her way. Her parents simply sighed, hoping age would cool her red-headed temper.

In this life, I was what today you would call an Irish Wolfhound. We were bred by her father Bran, who was considered the best dog breeder in all of Ireland. At that time, our uses were varied: some were trained for hunting large prey such as stags; others were trained to guard livestock; and still others were trained in the art of war: to run into the fray and take chunks from, or at least hamstring the enemy. Siblings from other litters had found their way into the packs of tribal chieftains and even the High King of Ireland, regardless of the political climate.

As I may have mentioned, Aoife was headstrong. And, like all my humans, quite smart. When she was nine, a Druid came to the homestead, called, he said, by a child from within their household. That evening as he gave the adults what news he had, he observed the family. Immediately after breakfast the next morning before everyone left for chores, Aoife's parents, revering the Druids like most others of their time, lined their children up from oldest to youngest for Dalaigh to inspect. It only took a minute for his eyes to light on Aoife who, instead of standing at attention as one did when being presented to elders, ignored him in favor of giving me a much-needed scratch behind my ears.

"This child I will take with me to the grove. With your permission, of course," Dalaigh pronounced.

Deidre, Aoife's mother, frowned. "Are you certain, sir? This one is a handful. I do not see her gaining the patience needed for your studies. Aedan, on the other hand, has already learned much of the trees surrounding our farm."

Dalaigh waved her cares aside. "I am sure. I see great things for this one."

Deidre shrugged her shoulders. "Then, Aoife, gather your things. You are going to live with this man's people and learn many things."

"I admonish you to pay attention to your studies. Do not bring shame upon this house and my name," Bran sternly told her.

Unsure of how to react to an abrupt change in her situation, Aoife for once was speechless. But she obeyed her parents and gathered her meager belongings together into a small bundle. She approached Dalaigh with apprehension, which was evident by the set of her shoulders and scowl on her face. One thing concerned her more than anything else.

"Sir, may I bring my dog?" Aoife inquired of Dalaigh.

"With your parents' permission, of course." Dalaigh knew what I was, but the niceties still had to be observed. Bran granted permission for me to accompany Aoife (we were already inseparable, as you might imagine) and we set off. We walked for two days, Aoife peppering Dalaigh with questions the entire time. Sleep was about the only thing that quieted her tongue, yet Dalaigh patiently answered everything he was able. Toward the end of the second day, the Druids' grove came into sight.

The grove, despite current lore, wasn't a just a circle of oak trees. Yes, there was that, but it was also what you would probably refer to as a school for gifted children. Each of the twenty or so children was allowed to bring their pet, which was interesting given that most animals had a function around a homestead, whether for hunting, guarding livestock, or keeping rats out of a barn. Most families would not have parted with such assistance. I later learned that the handful of Druids who traveled looking for these children had the gift of foresight. They were able to tell whether a child would manifest magic, what their element would be, and that each "pet" was a familiar. Where a family was reluctant to part with a useful dog or cat, the Druid either used his or her powers of persuasion, or money changed hands.

For six long years, Aoife spent hours memorizing poems (some of history, some set to music), recipes for healing potions, astronomy and how to interpret the stars, and the Brehon laws. The Druids knew what her element would be but not where her interests or strengths would lie. Therefore, she started training in all three disciplines.

The Druids discovered she needed discipline not only in their arts but with her temper. Rather than argue with her mouth, she did it more often with her fists. The healer threatened to name her hut after Aoife due to the number of scraped knuckles and bloody noses she had to treat. Aoife did eventually learn to debate rather than fight, but it was clear to others of her age that she was not to be messed with. As a result, she became something of a loner.

Life was not all classroom study. The grove was a small village that, like all villages in its time, was self-supporting. The children were expected to help with chores such as tending cattle and sheep, planting and weeding food gardens, and gathering healing plants that grew wild in the valley and higher up in the mountains. Because I was a dog and Aoife had no patience for gardening, we were tasked with helping with the animals – I would warn them if wolves or elk were near enough to threaten.

The children also partook in the seasonal festivals, which were also religious holidays. They may not have had class on these days, but there was always something to do.

At fifteen, her magic manifested – and not in a good way. She was, naturally, arguing with a teacher about some fine point of Brehon law, lost her temper and caused the roots of the tree the instructor was leaning against to curl up and embrace said teacher. Thankfully, it was not fatal, but her instructor bore marks on his face and arms for many years.

I began my job by, once again, giving her headaches (even though I tried to be gentle) until she learned who and what I was and accepted my presence in her mind. Thankfully, that came quickly because her teachers knew what was happening. I was also able to put a damper on her temper, for which many people were grateful.

At sixteen, she had her first vision. We were in class, Aoife learning how to process plants into healing mixtures and me gnawing on an elk bone, listening to Aoife think about how dumb this class was. All of a sudden, her thoughts turned from grumbling to an image of the grasslands where the sheep and cattle grazed. The young man who was supposed to be watching the herd appeared to be asleep, and there were several men creeping out from the woodland that edged the grazing area.

The Druids' grove, which belonged to no tuath, or kingdom, was set apart, much like your churches today belong to no country. *Most* people revered the Druids and rather than take something from them, gave gifts. These men obviously were not most people and were set to steal cattle, as was common at that time. Aoife was perplexed - how had her grumbling turned to such a horrifying thought?

Realizing this was no dream but reality, I nudged Aoife to tell her teacher what she saw. Naturally, she could not be polite and raise her hand to get the Druidess' attention but simply interrupted and blurted everything out. That, at least, conveyed the urgency of her message. Aoife was asked if she was certain, and I encouraged her to nod.

The teacher hurriedly dismissed class and raised the alarm. Every adult and teenager grabbed a spear or sling and raced toward the field, which was probably a normal fifteen-minute walk. The swiftest arrived in less than five minutes.

Aoife's warning was timely. Lorcan, the boy supposedly watching the herd, had been knocked unconscious. His hound was lying at his side, also unconscious, which explained the lack of canine alarm. The rustlers were in the process of rounding up the cattle when the first villagers arrived. At first, the thieves fought back, but as more people appeared and they found themselves outnumbered, they disappeared into the woods from which they had come, leaving one of their dead compatriots behind.

So it was that Aoife was declared a seeress and much to her delight, she was excused from all classes except those pertaining to divination and the Brehon laws. When she grumbled about the law class, it was explained to her in terse terms that *everyone* had to know the laws and how they were applicable to their area of study.

What she did not realize is that divination included not just visions but astronomy; what you would call ornithology, because they divined by bird call and flight, and one had to know the different birds, calls, and flight patterns; meteorology, because they studied weather patterns; dream interpretation; and casting sticks with marks on them, known as Ogham.

What do you mean, sticks? How did they figure out what they meant? Oh, wait. You mean like I Ching? I've heard of that.

Yes, similar to the I Ching, or even casting runes, or laying out cards such as your friend Cassandra does. Just a different system.

Okay.

As you probably know, there were no books. All subjects were taught by rote memorization. The teacher would recite something, and the class repeated it. *Ad nauseum* until the subject was drilled into the students' brains. This is perhaps why their schooling took twenty long years.

I learned right along with her. Some things a familiar instinctively knows but others, like the Druids' particular ways of doing things, we do not. Aoife excelled at ornithomancy, and although the dog preferred to chase the birds, I forced down the natural inclination and observed and remembered with Aoife.

At the age of thirty, Aoife was declared a fully-trained seeress and given her choice of life: either travel, as did Dalaigh, to find the exceptional children or be assigned to a nobleman as his personal diviner. She chose the latter, for which I was glad. Wolfhounds may be able to run fast, but we are sprinters, not marathoners.

Rather than living in a nobleman's house, Aoife found a place with Tierney, a Brehon, or judge. Unfortunately, he was the traveling sort, unattached to any king or tribal chieftain. Some forty years older than Aoife, he was a wizard, which explained his longevity in an era when achieving the age of seventy was considered a rare feat. The vast majority of people saw a man in the prime of his life, meaning around the age of thirty.

Tierney was pleased to have found a seeress to accompany him on his rounds. As an Air wizard, he used his magic to keep a calm atmosphere when he was judging cases. (It also came in handy for 'airing out' closed rooms with sweaty, nervous bodies. The Celts did bathe, but nothing could be done for the stench when a lot of bodies occupied an enclosed space in the winter.) He may have known the Fénechas, or Laws, backward and forward, but to have someone able to divine whether a petitioner or witness was telling the whole truth was a bonus. In addition, Aoife was, on occasion, able to see small details of the disagreement which the petitioner or witness may have overlooked and were pertinent to the case. Ask any policeman today, and they will tell you five people seeing the same accident will give five different versions of it. He or she must blend the statements into a cohesive whole picture of the event. Some things do not change over the centuries.

So, for the next twenty-plus years, we traveled a prescribed route through the countryside, staying first at this chieftain's house, then that minor king's. Tierney would arbitrate arguments the chieftain either could not decide or did not want to get involved with. Aoife would use her divination to aid in the decision and once in a while, do a reading for the chieftain or a member of his tribe. It was not a bad life. While we were on the road and between stops, I was allowed to give the dog free rein, hunting rabbits and other small animals for their evening dinner.

On occasion, Tierney was called to be a part of an appellate court. One such court was convened at Tara. It was the court of the *Ard Rí* or High King of Ireland. Tierney joined two others of his stature to determine whether the judgement of the king's brithem, or counselor, was correct.

While there, Aoife had a vision that involved the king in a nasty battle. As was right, she reported it to Tierney. In today's parlance, his reaction was, "And your point was…?" Fighting between tribes was almost an everyday occurrence. When Aoife gave him the meanings behind what she saw and told him she felt the battle was for the king's soul, Tierney felt this was something the king should probably know. Aoife was called to the throne, which was not a big chair in a castle but a smaller chair in a small enclosure around a large stone.

Lóegaire mac Néill stood and looked down from his height to Aoife. "So, you have had a vision about a battle for my soul. Tell me about it."

She related her vision once again, explaining the allegorical meanings behind objects and actions in the waking dream. The battle would take place sometime in the not-too-distant future, and his adversary, who followed a different god, would attempt to sway him from his belief in Crom, Lugh, Morrígan, and others.

Lóegaire's eyes narrowed. He admitted that he had heard of a new religion making its way into Britain and knew it was a matter of time before adherents of that faith made their way to Eire. Calling an old man to his side, he quietly conferred with him. During the conversation, both eyed Aoife, as if judging her. Which, if you think about it, is what kings did. Finally, the old man walked over to where we were standing.

Tadhg, the brithem, spoke to Aoife. "I am an old man even by our standards, and I do not see as well as I once did. The *Ard Rí* needs a seer at his side, especially if even more troubled times are ahead. He has asked that you join him and give him the benefit of your visions."

"I should ask Tierney, first," Aoife told him. "Technically, I am assigned to him."

Tadhg nodded. "Although he cannot overrule the *Ard Rí,* it is right that you at least inform him of the change."

Over the evening fire, Aoife related what had transpired to Tierney. "While I do not relish the thought of joining the High Court, it is my duty to help Lóegaire if I can. I am sorry to be leaving your company, though."

Tierney shrugged his shoulders. "I will admit that it has been nice having you along to verify the tales told, but as you say, it is a duty you cannot escape. I am leaving in the morning – the King has concluded his court. I wish you well in your endeavors and hope our paths cross again."

He rose and left the fire – presumably to gather his things then get some rest before starting back on the road in the morning. Aoife continued to stare into the flames, hoping to find a vision that would help her understand her new life. After a while, she realized nothing was coming, so went to her own bed.

Chapter Six

And so it was that Aoife became the personal seeress of the High King of Ireland. You must remember at that time, there were no castles such as Buckingham Palace. The king, his personal retinue, and army traveled around the country, mostly fighting against other kings in an attempt to conquer then hold lands. It was a brutal life.

Aoife and I were kept busy, looking for the most appropriate place to invade, which day would be good to start a skirmish, whether his next child would be a boy or girl... As her reputation for knowing trees spread, Aoife also oversaw the gathering of hazel nuts (which Tadhg swore were the reason for his longevity), the cutting of rowan branches for a new set of ogham staves (used even by lay people as a way to try and divine their own future), and even bow makers sought her out for advice on which yew branches would be best for a new bow.

Because of Aoife's status, we were never actually *in* any of the battles but kept behind the lines. Much to her chagrin, Aoife was tasked with helping the physicians. It was known all Druids were trained in rudimentary herbcraft and healing, so the King assigned her to helping with the wounded while went out and raged around with his sword. At least I did not have to bloody my muzzle on human flesh!

Although Tadhg continued to counsel Lóegaire until his death almost ten years later, for the most part, he left the seeing to Aoife. Many times Aoife and Tadhg would argue over the signs' meanings, and there were instances where I had to put a clamp on Aoife's temper. It was either that or she would have probably strangled Tadhg with tree roots or asked the ground to swallow him up.

True to Aoife's vision, a traveler visited the court about five years later at one of the quarterly meetings at Tara. He attempted to convince the king to renounce his multiple gods and convert to the traveler's faith, which recognized only one. The man was calm, polite-spoken but very insistent. He said something about his concern for the king's soul. The king laughed and vowed never to leave the gods who had given him his kingship. He offered the traveler food and a bed for the night, provided the man said nothing to anyone else about this new faith. The traveler declined and left the king's presence.

Aoife, of course, was standing by the king as this exchange took place. The traveler made her uncomfortable. Despite his soft-spoken ways, there was a warrior's aura about him. She had no doubt he would fight for his god and then wondered whether Lóegaire was as dedicated to his gods.

While a battle is a battle is a battle, all chaos and bloodshed, there was one interesting series. Although there were several kings who did not recognize Lóegaire's authority over them, the most troublesome one held sway over Leinster. As always with the Irish, cattle were involved. Lóegaire wanted a tribute, and Leinster refused to pay, so they fought.

One day, Leinster's troops managed to break through Lóegaire's lines and capture the king. Like most humans, when it came right down to it, he did not want to die. Leinster had become quite tired of Lóegaire's attempts to collect tribute, so after several heated exchanges between the two, Lóegaire vowed never to invade Leinster again, swearing the standard oath calling on all elements to witness. He was released back to his men, who seemed pleased he was essentially unharmed.

A year or two after that, the traveler found the king again and again asked him to convert to Christianity which, according to him, was the one true faith. This time, though, many of the king's followers (especially the wives of those followers) had converted, and he was pressured by them to accept the teachings of this Patrick fellow.

Aoife was called to the king's side and asked what the signs had to say about this Christianity. Aoife did not have to look to know the answer although at the king's insistence, she looked to the sky. Nothing she saw there was different than her logic had already told her. "This is a decision you must make for yourself, my lord."

Although I still do not understand it, I had come to realize that humans have a need to believe in something greater than themselves. So, Lóegaire's decision was not whether to believe at all, but what or who to believe in. Once again, the king refused to consider any god but those he had been raised with and sent Mr. Patrick away.

This caused some consternation in his court, and more than a few of his knights and such left because of it. The king took no action against them, as he felt everyone had a right to believe however they wished, despite the fact he thought they were wrong. Everyone else kept their opinions to themselves. The king's temper was legendary, although I privately thought his was nothing compared to Aoife's.

Life returned to normal. That is to say, exacting tribute of cattle from lesser kings, attempting to exact tribute by force from those who did not wish to pay it, and the quarterly gatherings at Tara.

It was at one of these gatherings that Lóegaire decided it was time Leinster came under his dominion once and for all. The old chief had died, and the son was deemed to be not as strong a leader. After the religious ceremonies and celebrations were over, he called his battle chiefs to his side and devised a plan he thought would finally bring that pesky place under control.

Aoife, who had become chief advisor after Tadhg's death, quietly reminded the king of his oath never to bother Leinster again. "My lord, you told me you swore an oath invoking the elements. Will you now violate something so sacred?"

"That oath was to another king. It does not hold with the new king."

Aoife shrugged her shoulders. Invoking the elements bound him to the land, not a person. But she knew better than to argue. So, she packed up her things and mounted her horse, riding alongside the king with his other advisors to Lóegaire's chosen place of conflict. I trudged next to Aoife. The army trudged behind.

The king led his troops down the River Boyne into the heart of Leinster territory. As we were marching along, a freak storm blew up. Normally gentle rain felt like arrows piercing the skin as it was blown sideways by the strong winds. Thunder crashed and lightning lit up the skies.

"It is a sign, my lord," Aoife shouted to be heard through the tempest. "You must withdraw."

"Nay, lass," the king bellowed. "'Tis but a storm and shall pass."

As soon as the final word left his mouth, a bolt of lightning struck the king on his horse. Aoife and I, along with several others and their horses, were thrown aside like rag dolls from the blast. With one last rumble of thunder, the wind died down, the rain subsided and off in the distance, one could see blue skies.

We picked ourselves up and assessed injuries. Everyone, including me, could hear nothing. Thankfully, I could hear Aoife's thoughts as she passed from one man to another. This one has burns, that one has nerve damage in his arm, the other one she did not know but he was unconscious. Our hearing slowly returned, and Aoife coordinated with the closest battle chief on which people needed to get to healers.

At the chief's orders, several of the king's men put together a makeshift litter with spears and blankets, and we started back in the direction from which we had come. The king's horse, which had also been killed by the blast, was stripped of its trappings and left for the vultures, which were never far from such a large group of humans who left plenty of detritus for them to feed on. Although the humans did not know it, vampires joined the vultures in cleaning up a mess from a battle. At the time, it was an easy way to get the blood they craved. And, more than one battle "casualty" rose to join their ranks.

I heard mumblings of "Taranis" from several of the advisors and even more of the regular army. It may have been their thunder god, or simply the elements taking revenge for a broken oath. At that point, it did not matter. Once we returned to the stone at Tara, the king's body was cremated in a huge pyre, and one of his sons was declared High King of Ireland.

After Aoife conducted Lóegaire's funeral, we slipped away from the gathering. Her thoughts were on leaving the High King's court - there was no love lost between her and the new king. It was easy to project a question into her mind, asking where we would go.

"At the moment, I am very tired of kings," she thought back to me. "I am also very tired of always moving from place to place. I have heard of a grove in the mountains to the southwest. Perhaps they will accept me. Maybe I could teach? I don't know. But I'd like to stay in one place. Maybe even marry and have a family."

I mentally snorted at this last. Who would want a woman with such a temper? However, because of that temper, I kept my opinion to myself.

Aoife formally took her leave of the new king, who did not seem sorry to see her go. She gathered her belongings, and as her horse was not hers but the king's, we set out on foot, seeking a new home.

It took us two years to find the grove she had heard of (or one like it in the same part of the country). Christianity may have been making good headway throughout the country, but there were still plenty of people who held to the old ways. Aoife's garb was, as was every Druid's, distinctive, and she was asked for readings all along our path. That meant we almost always had a roof over our heads at night, a hot meal for her, and as much meat as I could eat with my choice of bones to chew on.

The grove we found was very similar to the one Aoife came of age in. It was situated in the heart of mountains on the southwest coast of the country. As the High King's seeress, her reputation had spread and Aednat, the leader of the grove, welcomed her with open arms. Apparently, they did not have someone as well-versed in divination as Aoife, and she was indeed given the position of teaching that art. While she was with the children was the only time I saw her practice patience.

And much to my surprise, she met a man who could handle her temper! Ardan was a Druid, what you would call a bard. He played a stringed instrument and sang ballads, telling the history of man in general and Ireland in particular. He did not teach, but sang to the grove in the evenings. He also was generally the person who spoke with travelers, getting any news and eventually setting it to song to be memorized by the next generation of bards.

Ardan started pursuing Aoife almost as soon as we had settled into our new life. She, on the other hand, at slightly over one hundred years old, wanted little to do with the "young" man (he was only around sixty). At one point, he followed her through a vineyard, attempting to persuade her that he would be the perfect match for her. She became irritated and caused the vines to twine around his legs, stopping him in his path. (Actually, he fell on his face, but Aoife did not see that as she hurried away.) Despite her irascibility, Ardan did not give up his quest, and Aoife finally gave in after a couple of years. I do not believe she loved him, but it was a comfortable relationship that gave her the stability she craved.

Life was not without difficulty. The growing movement of Christianity had penetrated even our little corner of the world. The Druids who roved the country looking for magical children started being harassed instead of welcomed. The magical children who were once easily swayed to become Druids were now the "property of the Church," and we saw fewer and fewer come to live with us each year. This broke Aoife's heart. Although she had wanted children, she was unable to conceive and looked upon the youngsters she taught as her surrogate family.

We also had our share of priests and others come to the grove in an attempt to convert those who lived there. While they were not actively discouraged, it was made plain that the inhabitants did not intend to change their ways. While fewer children came to live at the grove, more adults did, seeking an escape from the persecution they faced in the outside world. Our grove became more and more isolated as the years went by; those seeking the Druids' assistance visited less and less.

Overall, however, it was peaceful, and Aoife lived with Ardan, teaching various forms of divination to whoever was interested, and giving readings to those who asked for them, for almost one hundred years. Only at the last did she decide she needed to "move on" and see something more of the mountains than just the view from the grove. After explaining her reasoning to Ardan, who took Aoife's explanation stoically, we left the grove and hiked farther up into the mountains.

Once again, I was able to give the dog free rein. I caught small animals and sniffed out wild vegetables for her meals. The only magic Aoife performed was to move tree branches to form a bower or scoop out some earth to make a small cave-like opening to protect us at night, all of which were returned to their natural state with thanks the next morning. Several weeks later, she took her last breath sitting on the ground with her hand on my back, leaning against a rock where she had a clear view of the infiniteness of the ocean.

Chapter Seven

I next opened my eyes to find a humungous eye staring down at me. "This one will do," said a voice coming from the direction of that eye. I was unceremoniously picked up and deposited into a dark something with small holes. The eye observed me through one of those holes.

I tested my new body. I was obviously quite small, with large hind legs, smaller front ones, two sets of wings, and feelers jutting from my forehead. As I moved the outer wings to test for flight, I made a noise. Curious, I tried it again. A slightly different noise emanated from my back. The eye staring at me, with its epicanthic fold, crinkled in delight.

If you are not familiar with insects, especially the *Gryllidae* family, I am describing a cricket. Not to put too fine a point on it, I was a *bug*. I had always thought my superiors infallible. How could they make such a huge mistake, putting the consciousness of a familiar into an insect's body?

I felt yet another metaphysical slap. "*We do not make such errors. Learn, youngling!*" My mind was filled with images, memories of others, I gathered. In five minutes, I had centuries' worth of history and knowledge crammed into my brain.

In less than five minutes, I could tell you I was in China and singing crickets were favored pets by not only the common people but nobility, as well. I believe they still are. The fact that I had been placed in a clay container rather than something fancier such as a small, gilded cage, told me my human was not even close to being upper class.

My body knew all the right moves, but my brain had some adjusting to do. In my previous three lives, I had been an animal that could easily adjust to human circadian rhythms. Crickets are

45

nocturnal. I slept during the day when my human was active and was awake during the night. My jar was on the floor next to her sleeping pallet. I presume my 'singing' lulled Hui, my human, to sleep.

Hui was a small child. Initially, I thought a toddler, but her language was more advanced. I later learned she was almost ten years old. Born under the sign of the Earth Rat (I will not go into detail, but you can certainly look it up on that thing you call the internet), she was a clever girl, confounding the adults with her ability to problem-solve...and get into trouble with the older children.

At the beginning, my life was rather boring. Sometime during the day, I was taken from my jar and placed into a small tube with air holes, which Hui tucked into a fold of her robe. It was warm there, and I almost immediately fell back asleep, until I was disturbed long enough to be put back into my jar. Once I fully awoke at nightfall, I observed that my jar had been cleaned, with new food (grains of boiled rice) and water put down for me. As I rubbed my wings together, singing her to sleep, I listened in on her thoughts of the day. They were largely concerned with what she had learned from her elders (mostly grain farming), the latest indignation perpetrated by one of her older brothers and wondering what it would be like to live in the Emperor's palace.

When autumn came, the crickets held by the other household occupants grew gradually quieter until there was no sound from them at all. Like all mundane crickets, they died when their season was done. I, on the other hand, continued my nightly song at full volume.

Apparently, that was taken as a sign, because with the first snowfall arrived a lady dressed in rich silks. Her hair was elaborately coiffed, and she wore cosmetics. Hui's parents were very deferential to her and hustled the children out of the main room into the sleeping quarters. All ten crowded the doorway, attempting to listen to the hushed conversation in the other room. The lady's head turned toward the children several times during the conversation, her eyes eventually settling on Hui. She rose and approached my human, squatting down so they could look each other in the eye.

"Hui, my name is Tian. Your parents are offering you a once-in-a-lifetime opportunity. You would come to live with me and my sisters in our house. There you will learn skills taught to few. You would dress as I do, eat food so rich it will take your tastebuds time to adjust, and meet wealthy and powerful people. Would you like that?"

Hui looked to her mother for guidance. The mother turned her head away. *So*, Hui thought. She had dreamed of living in the Emperor's palace, it was true. As a girl child, she really had no value to her parents. As a *small* girl child, she had even less. She was unable to do some things in the fields that her brother, two years younger than she was, could do. And the lady's clothes! She looked at her homespun robe. It held no comparison. Slowly and shyly with her eyes downcast, she nodded her head yes.

Tian smiled. "I had hoped you would say yes." She rose and went back to Hui's parents.

The mother told Hui to gather her things, including the cricket, and be ready to leave. As Hui turned to her pallet, she caught the exchange of a jingling pouch out of the corner of her eye. Hui straightened her shoulders, thinking she was off on an adventure none of her siblings would ever have.

I was put into the tube and tucked into my usual spot in Hui's robe. Through her eyes, I watched her bundle her extra clothing and my jar together into a small lump she could carry. An animal skin was thrown over her shoulders, and she tucked her feet into what could generously be called shoes, also made of animal skin. She marched into the main room and declared herself ready to go.

Peeking through one of my air holes, I watched as Tian ushered Hui into a palanquin. Furs were thrown over the women for warmth, the curtains closed and I felt us being lifted. It was *not* a smooth ride! While we were being jounced around, Tian quietly prepared Hui for her new life.

"We are approximately two days from our home," she began. "What do you know of geography?"

Hui shook her head. "I do not know this word."

Tian sighed. "I can see there will be more to your schooling than just our duties. We will begin. First, geography means to study the land and all its features. That includes not only your parents' fields and where you lived but where things are, like landmarks and cities, and what they are called.

"Our country, Zhongguo, or the Middle Kingdom, is the greatest on earth. It is so large, it would take us a lifetime and more to walk its borders. We live in a large, prosperous city called

Yangzhou. It is near the Grand Canal and has people from many countries living and trading there."

She continued at length, describing the scenery beyond the curtains, allowing Hui the occasional peek which let in a lot of cold air. I snuggled farther down into my tube where, against Hui's skin, it was much warmer, and slept.

I awoke to the light of a candle and the smell of cooked meat. I hoped there was rice being served with it – I was hungry! At some point I had been transferred from the traveling tube to my clay jar. Probing Hui's mind, I discovered we were at a small inn for the night, and the room she was sharing with Tian was larger than the house from which she had just departed. The food being placed before her was more than she was accustomed to eating all day. She was in awe.

The lid to my jar was lifted and a lump of boiled rice was placed next to my water dish. Tian's voice quietly said, "Never fear, little cricket. I know what you are and will ensure Hui takes good care of you until such time as she also recognizes you."

The lid was replaced, and I settled in to eat. I knew Hui was still young and I had a few years before her magic would manifest. We would learn of her new life together.

Shortly after leaving the inn the following morning, we were taken aboard a barge on the Grand Canal and ushered into a small room with no windows. It was explained that it would be warmer inside than even staying in the palanquin during our short voyage – it was a particularly harsh winter. So, there we stayed – I slept – for the better part of the day.

I was awakened once again by the smell of food. This time it wasn't just meat sizzling but spices! I looked out a hole in my jar to see an opulent room – silks lined the walls, the tables were highly polished wood and the cushions on which Hui and Tian sat were as exquisitely embroidered as Tian's dress. While I did not know Tian's profession, whatever it was, it was a preferable alternative to the hut Hui had come from.

Hui shared a room with Tian for the first several years. We were in a household with four other women all around the same age as Tian, and all witches with crickets as familiars. They all had male patrons who would visit on a regular basis, hosted parties for the men and the people they wanted to impress or, on occasion, the ladies would be called to the patron's home or to accompany him to the theater or wherever else it was necessary to have a lovely lady on your arm.

While Tian was her main teacher, all five women helped with the instruction of "Little Daughter." Hui learned to play music (she could not carry a tune to sing), to compose poetry, was taught table manners, how to read, how to discuss important matters of the day without actually putting forth an opinion, and how to comport herself around important men. However, much to my relief, she was not taught how to please those men in bed. She was being trained to be a Yiji –a companion, but nothing more.

Because the other crickets were familiars, I was able to quickly learn what went on in this particular household - and they taught me how to adjust my circadian rhythms to match those of my human.

At the time, China's official religion was Taoism. As such, the ladies were trained in its ethics. They also learned the I Ching, a form of divination, as you know. They were considered by many of their patrons to be spiritual advisors. Ya-Fen, whose element was Air, was quite adept at calming her patrons when something did not go their way.

Hui's magic erupted at age fourteen. As a trainee, it was her duty to observe (through a hidden hole in a wall) how the women entertained – and advised – their patrons. After pouring tea and playing her *dizi*, a kind of flute, Tian's patron still had not calmed from whatever had transpired during the day. He demanded she cast the stalks for him to find out why his transaction had not gone in his favor. She did and determined that his manner made him seem untrustworthy.

"I *am* trustworthy," he roared. "I would never do anything to imply otherwise. You must be *mistaken!*"

"I am sorry, my lord," Tian said quietly while bowing her head. "I only repeat what I see in the hexagram."

He howled again and this time, struck Tian so hard she flew across the room. Hui, unnerved by such a violent temper, wanted only to revenge the hurt done to her gentle mentor. As I watched, the polished ebony table rose and smacked the patron in the head.

Tian's eyes widened (as much as they could with the bruise forming next to her left eye) as she witnessed the magic. At the same time, Hong, the house guard, entered the room to see what all the noise was about.

"My lady, is there something wrong?" Hong asked as he helped Tian to her feet.

"I believe I can take care of the situation," Tian replied. "Please escort Ho-Xiansheng to the door. See that he does not ever return." Hong nodded and, grabbing the patron by the arm, hauled him to his feet and out the door. Tian faced the wall with the hidden hole.

"Little Daughter, I know you are watching. Please come in here so I may speak with you."

Hui rushed from one room to the other, nearly dislodging my tube from her dress. "Honored Sister, how may I help heal your face?"

"It is of no importance right now. The bruise will fade shortly. Do you know what you did?"

Hui felt confused. "I did nothing. But I did see the table rise of its own accord and hit Ho-Xiansheng."

"I believe you caused the table to rise. Did you feel anger when I was struck?"

"Yes, Honored Sister. I did not like to see you treated that way. He was wrong to hit you."

"Yes, he was wrong. But that is not your concern at the moment. I would like you to try to raise the table again. This time, just off the floor – do not throw it anywhere."

Hui was the one to widen her eyes. "How would I do that?"

"Concentrate. You know what ebony feels like to your hands. Find that feeling in your mind, and then just as if you would use your hands to lift the table, do it with your thoughts."

At last! I could finally work. I helped Hui to locate the table with her magic and then, slowly, lift the table a few inches off the floor. As the table rose, so did Hui's astonishment, and the table fell back to the floor with a thud.

"I did that?" Hui cried.

"Yes, Little Daughter, you did. We, the five of us women and now you, possess magic. I felt no air stirring, so I believe your ability is with Wood, as is mine. It is a skill few possess."

Wait. Wood is an element?

Yes. In Chinese astrology, Wood is one of the five elements, along with Water, Fire, Earth and Metal. They do not recognize Air, but most Air witches are considered to be of the Fire element. You know, they can use air to fan flames. As you have discovered, Earth witches can also easily manipulate wood and metal. Do not ask me to explain Chinese philosophy to you. We would be here for the rest of your life. Now, back to my story.

Hui massaged her temples. "I have a headache," she whimpered.

"It feels like someone pressed hard on your temples, does it not?"

Hui nodded.

"That will go away with time. The pressure you felt is your familiar helping you. We have much to speak of, but right now, I need to ask Li-Ting to heal my face. I will meet you in our room in a few minutes."

So began Hui's introduction to her magic. As a true Earth witch, she commanded earth and metal in addition to wood. But because of her mentor's philosophy, she concentrated on wood. Her instruction was augmented by Li-Ting, a healer whose element was Water but she was also an adept at herbal preparations.

Hui grew to be a beautiful woman. Not in the most desirable sense – full-figured women were fashionable at that time, and Hui did not have a lush figure. But there were men who preferred petite women, which Hui certainly was. She had taken all of her lessons to heart and with time, became one of the most popular Yijis in Yangzhou.

It wasn't her beauty that made her so popular, though. It was the music she made with her *dizi* – her bamboo flute. And the flutes she made herself. She knew which pieces of wood would resonate well and how to carve them to get the most beautiful sounds from them. What her patrons did not know is that she magically manipulated any tiny flaws in the wood that might detract from the tone.

In time, her flutes drew the attention of the emperor in Chang'An. One afternoon as Hui was preparing for a party in their home that evening, an emissary arrived at the door. Boqin, who had replaced Hong as the senior guard when he retired, ushered the emissary into the greeting room, backing out the door on his hands and knees.

Hui, however, knowing her status, refused to kowtow. "To what do I owe this pleasure, great sir?"

"His most majestic person has heard of your flutes and your music. He wishes your presence at court."

You must remember that a wish from an emperor was actually a command. Hui, however, had lost none of her feistiness over the years.

"Please tell his most august majesty that, although I am quite flattered, I am happy with my life here and have no wish to leave. I will, however, be pleased if you would take one of my creations with you as a gift."

At that moment, Tian entered the room. At the sight of the emissary, Tian's eyes widened but, like Hui, she would not kowtow. Instead, she chose to ignore him and asked, "Little Daughter, have you completed all the preparations?"

"I was about to, Honored Sister, when this man suggested I accompany him to court. It seems news of my flutes has reached the Emperor's ears and he wishes my presence. I offered to send a flute as a gift."

Tian gave the impression of thinking things over, although there wasn't much to think about when a command came from on high. It was just a matter of complying while maintaining the appearance that it was a choice.

"Little Daughter, it seems to me an opportunity to showcase your talents has arisen. I suggest you take advantage of it. Allow me to complete the party preparations while you gather such things as you think you will need for this journey."

Tian called for a servant and instructed her to make the emissary comfortable while Hui packed. The two ladies departed the greeting room and made their way to the room they still shared.

"This is indeed a fortunate occurrence for you," Tian murmured. Bamboo walls did nothing to prevent sound from travelling. "I suggest you pack very lightly and allow the Empress to robe you appropriately for your presentation. One trunk should suffice for your flutes and a little clothing."

Twenty minutes later, one of the emissary's footmen carried the trunk and strapped it to the back of a luxurious horse-drawn coach. Hui quickly said her farewells to her housemates (truly hoping she would return quickly) and with me tucked into her robes, we began our journey to court.

Chapter Eight

Our trip to the capital was quite similar to the one which brought us to Yangzhou. The carriage took us to the Grand Canal, where we boarded one of the Emperor's personal barges. The accommodations were considerably more luxurious than our previous trip. We spent three days on the Canal, listening to the emissary describe the sites to Hui as we flowed past them.

The emissary, Chang, was actually from the Empress' household. It was the Empress who had heard of Hui's music and decided to bring her to court, but anything from court was officially from the Emperor. He was educated and pleased to have a travelling companion who could converse intelligently.

We finally left the barge mid-afternoon on the fourth day and were taken once again by horse-drawn coach to the palace, which was visible from the dock because it sat high above on a small plateau. We disembarked in the courtyard of a small city, one that seemed to still be under construction. Through Hui's eyes, I was able to take in the magnificence of the complex known as Hanyuan Palace. Chang ushered us quickly through the doors of a small building attached by corridors to several larger ones, the footman following with Hui's trunk.

That evening, Chang escorted her through a series of winding hallways to the Empress' apartments, Hui attempting to keep up while being weighed down by the elaborately jeweled and embroidered robe sent for her to wear. Physically left in her room, I rode along in Hui's mind, determined to keep her calm. Any nerves would have shown in her playing. My life was just as much in jeopardy as hers!

At the door to the Empress' apartments, both removed their shoes and got down on their knees. Chang slid the door open, and as he did, both lowered their heads to the floor. "I bring the lady Hui as you requested, oh Magnificent One," Chang announced.

"You may enter," a melodious voice answered. Both scuttled into the room, still on their knees, still with their heads nearly on the ground. As Chang slid the door closed behind them, the voice said, "Oh, goodness. We're not in the throne room. At least raise your heads so I can see what the child looks like."

Hui sat back on her haunches and raised her head to look at the Empress, although as a Yiji, she had been trained to look at someone without looking them directly in the eye. She saw a woman, perhaps in her sixties, dressed in what to Hui's eyes were the most elaborate robes she had ever seen. The Empress frankly appraised her.

"You are a small one, aren't you? Well, well, size does not matter, as I've told other emperors. Play something for me." Wu Zetian reclined in her cushions, obviously expecting to be entertained.

With a sidelong glance to Chang, Hui played a song she knew Tian had used to soothe upset clients. I believe the lyrics were about birds and sunsets but, of course, Hui did not sing them. Instead, remembering what Chang had said about the Empress having a bad day, she infused a little of the calming energy she had learned into her playing.

When the last note died away, the Empress sighed. Hui tensed, and although I tried to keep her calm, I tensed right along with her. This was what you would today refer to as a 'make or break' moment.

"That was lovely. Play something else. Play several somethings else."

After almost an hour, Hui laid her flute in her lap and looked expectantly at the Empress. Quietly, she said, "I am sorry, Magnificent One, but I have played as much as I can tonight and still retain the ability to play tomorrow. May I return tomorrow evening and play more for you, then?"

Another 'make or break' moment. In the outside world, Hui was well within her rights to quit when she felt ready. At Court, however, one did not normally stop doing whatever until told to do so.

We thought the Empress had fallen asleep, but she did not start at the cessation of music or Hui's question. Slowly opening her eyes, she eyed Hui. For an agonizing several minutes. Finally, she spoke.

"First, you may address me as 'Your Highness.' Chang's affectations need not rub off on you. Second, the answer to your question is yes, but it will be later in the evening. Thirdly," she turned to Chang, "make this person one of my household and put her in with the other ladies. Arrange to have her things brought from wherever you put them." She looked at Hui again. "We will speak tomorrow evening."

They were dismissed. I tried to mentally caress Hui as a sign of my approval – and relief. Hui and Chang bowed again and scuttled backward out the door. Once in the hall, Chang blew out a breath. "Come."

That evening, Hui mused on this turn in her life. Obviously, the move from her parents' to Yangzhou was a good one, but to Court? Although she preferred to return to Tian and the others, one simply did not say 'no, thank you' to the ruthless mother of the ruler of your land. (She had already deposed one of her sons and replaced him with a grandson.)

I sent reassuring thoughts. The Universe meant for us to be here at this time. And, frankly, there was nothing she could do about it without losing her head!

The following evening saw *us* once again in the Empress' apartments. I was comfortably ensconced in my tube hidden in the folds of Hui's robe. Which, by the way, was not quite as elaborate as the one she had worn the previous night.

After Hui had played two songs, the Empress interrupted her as she was about to begin the third. "So, my child, you have the gift of music. What other gifts do you bring to me?"

Hui was puzzled. "Highness? What do you mean?"

The Empress laughed. "Oh, child. Do you think Chang did not do his research after word of you reached Us? What Element do you control?"

We were flabbergasted. Magic, while accepted, was not spoken of in polite circles. The official Taoism practiced by those of the Tang Dynasty was one of meditation techniques to achieve harmony with the Universe, and magic was usually in the form of talismans and alchemy. To have *real* magic spoken of, even in the privacy of the Empress' apartment, was akin to heresy.

55

"Highness? I do not know how to answer you," Hui quietly but firmly stated. Was she being tested? To what end? And how was she to answer such in a room populated by not only the Empress but her retainers?

Another low, quiet laugh. "You may speak freely in this room. This is why." Wu Zetian slowly raised her right arm. One of the servants rose from the ground, still in her crouched position. While holding the servant off the ground, the Empress nodded at another retainer (Hui thought he was a scribe), who held out his palm and a small flame appeared. He smiled at Hui and closed his palm around the flame, extinguishing it.

Wu Zetian lowered the servant, who had not batted an eyelash, back to the floor. "As you can see, private reality can be different than the public face. So, to reiterate, what Element do you control?"

Hui demonstrated by raising the ebony table on which the Empress' Jin Dynasty tea set was displayed. Not a single piece of porcelain moved as the table rose and then settled back on the floor as light as a feather.

"Ah, I presume Wood? Which would explain your marvelous flutes."

Hui inclined her head. "Yes, Your Highness."

The Empress' eyes glittered. "And can you imbue wood with properties, not just move it?"

"Yes, Your Highness."

"Excellent. I will have work for you on occasion. In the meantime, play some more of your beautiful music."

So began our introduction to Court. One unfortunate aspect of living at Court was the politics and behind-the-scenes machinations and oh, there was plenty to go around. At this time, the Emperor, Ruizong, was a figurehead only. He never appeared at Court functions and kept to his own apartments. Wu Zetian ruled the land.

Hui was ordered to resume her duties as Yiji but this time as a spy for the Empress. Hui was to accompany officials or minor sons to one function or another then report back, which went against all Hui's training. However, when Hui protested, her air supply was abruptly cut off.

"Do not attempt to thwart me," the Empress warned. "You are mine to do with as I wish. And I wish you to find out what is happening behind my back. Be thankful I do not ask you to sleep with them."

Hui's oxygen was restored and, gasping for breath, she bowed. "Of course, Your Highness. I will do as you ask." As if there was anything else to do and still live.

For the next several years, Hui played her flute at Court; accompanied men to dinners, plays and such; and spoke with Chang regarding what she had overheard here and there. As promised, Hui's magic was also used in the Empress' service. One "specialty" was that carved wooden figurines would be imbued with poison, enchanted to splinter at a particular time, and then gifted to the Empress' enemies. Hui had nothing to do with the carving or poison, but she was instructed to cause the splintering when the figurine came into contact with the target. Therefore, she was complicit in several deaths, which did not sit well with either of us.

Four years into our stay at Court, Wu Zetian apparently tired of being a regent and administrator, and Ruizong officially yielded the throne to her. As an aside, she became the only female emperor in China's history.

Shortly after taking the throne, Wu elevated Buddhism to the official religion, probably at the behest of her long-time lover, a Buddhist monk. Meat could once again be eaten at Court! Although she did not like the monk personally, Hui was grateful that she could finally eat animal flesh, and dug into her first piece of roast cow with relish.

Hui was relieved of her duties as a spy and made a lady-in-waiting. Her duties were to ensure the Empress' comfort and safety. Gifts were always arriving. If they were made of wood, Hui inspected them for any anomalies. Many were found – the Empress and her household were not the only ones who employed magic – and the senders were either executed or taken as slaves.

A month after Wu took the throne, Chang gifted Hui with a tea set made of jade.

"Use this set when entertaining anyone you do not trust," he told her. "I have imbued it with the ability to sense danger. If your guest means you harm, it will chime as a bell in your hearing only when the cup is picked up."

"It's lovely and I thank you, but why?" Hui asked.

Chang blushed a little. "A selfish reason. I like you, and I like your music. I would not wish something bad to happen to you."

Three years later, that tea set probably saved our lives. As I said before, intrigue and political maneuvering was a fact of daily life. Hui roomed with three other ladies-in-waiting, one of whom, Wei Tuan, was a cast-off lover of Li Dan, the heir apparent. Hui knew despite her efforts to remain as far in the background as possible (and therefore draw little attention to herself) that she was one of Wu's favorites. This elicited jealousy from various parts, including Wei Tuan, who was also a favorite.

After ensuring the Empress was asleep and would not rise again until mid-morning, Hui and her roommates had a ritual of enjoying a cup of chamomile tea together before they, too, retired. It was Hui's turn to make the tea and on a whim, drew Chang's tea set out from her trunk to use rather than their standard fired clay set.

As Hui served them, the other ladies exclaimed over the beauty of the set, wondering who would gift her something so valuable. It was known Hui was no one's consort, and they did not know if she had a lover (she did not). Hui simply said it was from an admirer and left them in the dark.

From my cage, I was able to observe the goings-on much better than from my tube in Hui's robes, where I only saw what she saw. Chinese women are no different than any others: they talk and gesture so much that it takes them some time to actually drink any of their beverage. As a consequence, none of them drank at the same time.

As Wei Tuan took her first sip, we heard the chime of a bell. Hui looked around, wondering where the sound had come from. I projected an image of Chang enchanting the tea set in her mind, then flashed another image of Wei Tuan. That was enough to get her attention as to what was happening.

Knowing full well that nothing could happen in their quarters (Wu would have just executed the remaining three if something happened to the fourth), Hui slept soundly. The following day, after seeing the Empress to the Throne Room and withdrawing, Hui paid a visit to Chang in his office as principal secretary to the Empress.

"Your tea set chimed last night," she told him. "I know who, but I do not know from which quarter the danger will come. Therefore, I do not know what to guard against."

Chang bade her sit. "I probably already know who. Wei Tuan, correct?"

Hui nodded. She knew Chang had spies not only in every quarter of the palace but virtually every quarter of the country. Some for the Empress' benefit, of course, but many more for his alone.

"Do not fear. Wei Tuan has overstepped herself once in an effort to get revenge against Li Dan. I have it on good authority she is about to do so again. I believe it's time for her to leave court permanently, don't you?"

Hui shuddered. She detested the political machinations and resulting executions. Wu was nothing short of bloodthirsty at times. "I do not wish harm to anyone, but least of all myself. If yours is the only way…"

Chang patted her on the shoulder. "Go back to your duties. I will take care of everything."

Hui turned to leave, then stopped and looked back at Chang. "Before I leave, may I ask you a question?"

"Of course."

Hui screwed up her courage and asked what she had been wanting to know almost since the day Chang escorted her to Court. "You have always been so kind to me, including the gift of the tea service, which I know was not inexpensive. Yet you have never asked anything of me. Not even to take me as a lover. Why?"

Chang guffawed. "Oh, child. Has no one told you in all these years? I am a eunuch! Wu had me castrated the day I came into her service some fifty years ago. She said it was to ensure that no other woman would ever claim my loyalty."

He sighed. "I will admit to missing the company of a lovely lady and were I able to do so, I would have asked you years ago. Now, I can only be a friend. You are so pretty, and the fact that you make no pretensions to being anything but what you are makes you even more attractive. And, frankly, it's nice to have a friend who doesn't want to use you for anything. I have my fill of that in my position as principal secretary. Promise me you won't change?"

Hui, in an uncharacteristic display of affection, hugged him. "I do not know how to be anything but what I am, so I believe I can keep that promise. Promise me one thing?"

Chang inclined his head. "If I can."

"I know you love all the intrigue. Please do not get caught, much less executed. If that were to happen, I would lose the only person I know to be a true friend."

Chang hugged her, then noticed a thrush had entered the room through an open window. He listened for a moment, then bowed as the thrush departed.

"I value my own life, so I can promise I will take all precautions. But as you know, there are no guarantees at Court! Now, back to the Throne Room with you. I am told the Empress has nearly concluded her public meetings for today."

Chapter Nine

True to his word, Chang arranged it so someone else dropped a dime, as you would say, on Wei Tuan. It happened two nights later, as the Empress was speaking to three of her chancellors about a possible uprising in another part of the country. Chang sat at a writing cabinet in one corner, taking notes as needed. The ladies, as was the requirement, sat quietly in another corner, waiting to be called for one need or another. Although Wu and her chancellors spoke in low voices, a word or two occasionally reached the ladies' ears. Several, on this occasion.

"Your Highness, one of my spies tells me this uprising has its roots here in the palace," a particularly haughty man said. "I have names, if you would like to interrogate them."

Wu stared at the man. "How do you know your spy to be truthful, and how did he or she get these names you offer me?"

"He is a retainer in one of your sons' households, Your Highness. And the man offered to slit his own belly if I found him to be in error."

Wu snorted. "Everyone says that. Give me the list. I will have it checked out. Now, I am tired. You all may leave. I will send for you when I am ready to reconvene tomorrow." She waved her hand in dismissal, and the three chancellors filed out.

Wu thrust the scroll at Chang. "Check this out. Tell me what you find in the morning." She turned to the ladies. "I wish to retire. Hui, go get one of your flutes. I want to fall asleep to your music."

Chang winked at Hui as she passed by him on her way to get a flute. So, Chang had quickly arranged something. Hui felt bad but at the same time relieved. As did I.

61

The following afternoon, the same people were sitting in the same room, discussing the same subject.

"Chang, do you have that list?" Wu demanded.

Chang retrieved the scroll and gave it to her. "I have made notations next to each name, Magnificent One. You will see that I could only implicate three of the twenty."

Wu scanned the notations. Her eyes grew cold. "Wei Tuan…"

Wei's eyes grew large, and she bowed her head to the floor. "Yes, Your Highness? How may I serve?"

"You may serve me by falling on someone's sword. Now."

Wei's eyes got even larger, if that was possible. She stuttered, "Your Highness? Why?"

Wu said nothing more to her, simply instructed the guards to take her away. They moved toward our corner, and Wei saw what was coming. She attempted to flee out a conveniently located door but Hui, seeing what was happening, caused the flooring to part and trap one of Wei's ankles. When the guards were able to grab Wei, she released the ankle and returned the floor to its original composition.

The guards, a part of Wu's personal staff, knew the ladies well. "Thank you, Hui," one of them said. Naturally, nothing came from the direction of the Empress. Wei glared at Hui as she was dragged from the room. We never heard of her again.

Life for the next few years was routine, at least as far as Hui was concerned. Check wooden gifts, play her flutes, pour tea, lay out robes. Despite magic generally keeping one young, the Empress was starting to age rapidly. She dropped the Buddhist monk and took an imperial physician as a lover. In addition, soothsayers (none of whom had magic) were brought into her personal circle. Chang was demoted from a close personal advisor to simply a secretary.

"She is not in her right mind," Chang confessed to Hui over a late dinner one night. "She is drinking teas concocted by her lover rather than a wizard herbalist, and no one knows what is in them. She is listening to these charlatans more than her long-time advisors. It is not good, not good at all."

Hui, knowing all that was happening, tended to agree. "But there is nothing we can do about it, is there? Especially now that you are out of her inner circle."

Chang sighed. "I know. I just worry. I do not like not knowing what is happening!"

Hui smiled at him. "There you are, trying to arrange everything. How about arranging your affairs in case something happens to her?"

"*That,* my dear, has been arranged for a long time. I am waiting to see who she names as her successor before putting my plans into action. They do include you, you know."

Hui stared at him. "Me? What? And…without asking me?"

Chang patted her on the shoulder as he was wont to do. "I would – and will – ask you when the time is right. Everything very much depends on who her successor is and his disposition. Will we be kept on?"

Hui knew close servants were usually executed when a monarch died, and she certainly did not relish that fate. However, she would trust Chang. How could she not?

Several months later, Wu named her son as her successor, relinquished her throne to him and a day later, left for one of the outlying palaces. At that point, Wu was so ill that only her physician lover and a select handful of servants accompanied her. (Servants selected by the lover, all of whom were without magic.) As soon as Wu was carried out of her apartments, Chang was at Hui's side with one of his servants.

"Gather your things quickly and meet me in my apartment. Hu will carry what you cannot. There is no time to lose."

Without questioning him, Hui hurried back to her shared room with Hu in tow. Thankfully, Hui was a neat person, and it took no time at all to put a few comfortable robes into her trunk, along with the tea set and her flutes. Hu picked up the trunk, Hui grabbed an outer robe and my cage, and we took back passages to Chang's apartment.

"Good, you came quickly," Chang breathlessly greeted her. "Come."

He led her to the back corner of his sleeping room where Hu stood with two other men and a pile of trunks. Hu pulled up a corner of the floor which revealed … bricks. Hui looked at Chang with a question in her eyes.

Chang smiled. He moved his hands in front of him as if he were swimming the breaststroke, and the bricks seemingly melted to each side, *now* showing a sloping tunnel. Obviously, the servants already knew what to do, because they each picked up a trunk and headed down the passage.

Chang gestured, "After you, my dear."

There was nothing to do but follow. The tunnel was not steeply sloped but continued down for several paces before leveling out. It was wide enough for the tall-ish, broad-shouldered servants to walk without fear.

"What's happening? Where are we going?" Hui asked.

Hui felt a pat on her shoulder from behind. "Hush. I'll explain it all when we are on the other side of the palace gates. Not before." They continued on in silence, once turning themselves sideways so the servants could go back for the rest of the trunks.

About ten minutes later, we emerged into a small, dank storage room lit only with a badly smoking torch. Were I able to sneeze, I would have. Three trunks were already on the dirt floor in front of us. Chang pulled Hui to one side as Hu and the other two servants came huffing down the passageway with the remaining belongings. As the last one crossed the threshold, Chang swept his hands together and the tunnel closed, leaving no trace.

"Magic comes in handy at times, does it not?" Chang winked at Hui.

Hu had stuck his head outside the one door. "Carriage is here."

"Come, my dear. Let's have a little adventure, shall we?" Chang guided Hui out the door and into a nice but nondescript carriage pulled by two nice but nondescript horses.

They made themselves comfortable inside the carriage while it bumped and jumped as the trunks were loaded and strapped to the top. Chang reached into a corner and pulled out a stoppered bottle as we felt the coach start away.

"Tea? It isn't hot but should be refreshing after our rather dusty walk."

"Thank you," Hui said after she'd taken a sip. "Will you now tell me what is happening and where we're going?"

Chang cleared his throat, took another sip from the bottle then replaced the stopper. "Wu, or should I say someone using her chop, issued an edict three days ago naming Li Xian as emperor. As you are aware, Wu has left for one of the outlying palaces where I suspect she will live out her days, however many may remain to her. There is no love lost between Li Xian and me. Never has been. Once I learned of the edict, I also learned he planned to have Wu's entire staff put to the sword as soon as she was out of the palace and would not see. It was time to put my plan into motion.

"You have never been alone these last three days, so there was no time to say anything to you. If you do not approve of my plans, I will ensure you are somewhere safe and happy. But…"

"But what?" Hui was getting upset. I had the utmost regard for the eunuch and sent calming energy to her.

Chang's eyes twinkled. "I believe you will be happy in the life I have chosen. We are on our way to Yangzhou which, I believe, you are familiar with."

Hui was elated. "You are taking me home to Tian and the others?"

"Home to Yangzhou, yes. To your former house, no. I regret to tell you they are no longer there, and I do not know where they have gone. I did look for them."

Hui was crestfallen. "So…?"

"As you know, I have my fingers in many cakes and have made quite a bit of money, trading not only information but goods. Once Wu started her decline, I consolidated my merchant enterprises into a house in Yangzhou and have been operating it remotely. With the assistance of trusted friends, of course. We have let it be known that the owner, me, is not happy with my friends' fiscal performance, so I am returning to put things to rights in person."

Hui interrupted. "Why are you lowering yourself to become a merchant? With your connections, couldn't you simply ally yourself with another family?"

Chang shook his head. "I am too well known as Wu's creature for anyone in aristocratic circles to accept me, especially while Li Xian is in power. No, I prefer to begin a new life, with a new name, away from Chang'an or any other Imperial city. Changing social class is nothing *if* you have all the comforts you wish, which I do.

"Now, no one knows you are coming with me, but I would be happy to introduce you as my wife, my consort, whatever you want. If you wish, I can set you up in your own Yiji house."

Hui thought for a moment. Resuming her career as a Yiji, while not the same as a prostitute, would mean almost more of the same as she had endured at Court: listening to men plot and plan, and pretending to be sympathetic to them. But she was not trained for anything else. I had to interrupt that train of thought. Yes, she was, she just was not thinking in that direction. I projected an image of her flutes into her mind. Knowing she would not be able to *play* them forever, I immediately followed that with an image of her hands carving a flute.

Hui projected back gratitude. "I do not wish to return to a life as a Yiji. You may like all the plotting, but to be honest, it's tiresome. Even while I was in training, I wondered how Tian could endure listening to her clients without a single sigh.

"I do, however, enjoy my flutes. Perhaps I could make them and you could sell them for me?"

Chang frowned. "Even before you came to Court, your musical talents were known. If Li Xian were to hear of you, I can assure you his retainers would swiftly wipe out the last of Wu's known ladies."

He paused, gave her a long, appraising look and brightened. "*But*! How would you feel about being a boy?"

Hui choked. "What?"

"Because I was castrated relatively late in life, or late in life if I was fully human, I do not have all the physical attributes of someone who had their testes removed before puberty. Therefore, only a few people are aware of my status. You, my dear, as pretty as you are, could pass for a boy if you did not wear female robes or use cosmetics, and if you cut your hair.

"As a male *and* as my purported lover, you would have more freedom of movement and artistic expression than you would appearing as you do now. Li Xian and his cohorts wouldn't bat an eyelash at a boy carving marvelous flutes and his successful merchant lover selling them."

After this statement, Hui was choking so hard her face was red. Chang handed her the flask with a grin on his face. Hui attempted not to gulp the liquid as she thought furiously. The more she thought, the more it sounded like a good idea. Women, unless they were a member of the aristocracy, were only slightly more regarded than slaves. Even the male slaves in the palace were better treated than the females. The idea had merit, but in execution?

"What about Hu and your other servants? They already know me as a woman."

"Well, first of all, Hu is the only one with a tongue. I rescued Da and Gang from Li Zhi's household. He'd taken offense at something someone else overheard and reported, and had their tongues removed. Then the fact that they couldn't say 'yes' while kowtowing irritated him, and they were going to be executed. With Wu's permission, I brought them into my household.

"Hu is the soul of discretion. He knows almost all *my* secrets, and I am still very much alive. Therefore, it's obvious he doesn't tell tales. I think your secret would be safe with them."

Hui's thoughts were a jumble. "Your idea has merit, but changing my whole identity? I need to think about this."

A 'thump' came from the direction of the driver's foot. "I understand," Chang said as he peeked out the carriage window. "I believe we're coming to our destination for the evening. Why don't you sleep on it, and we'll speak again tomorrow?"

They spent the night at the house of a friend of Chang who, very obviously, was also a eunuch. No introductions were made, just the standard formal greetings exchanged. As soon as they had eaten, Chang and his friend disappeared into another room and were not seen again until morning. Servants saw to Hui's comfort. She was awake a good portion of the night, thinking about her circumstances. I tried my best to lull her to sleep with my song and calming energy, but her mind was too occupied. I eventually gave up and was able to fall asleep. At least one of us should be awake and alert the next day.

The following day saw them back in the carriage. "Well? Have you thought about my proposition?" Chang asked almost as soon as the carriage started rocking.

"I have. It sounds possible, but I have several questions. First of all, a boy that never grows? I have no facial hair and will never have any. I will not get any taller. My voice will never deepen. Won't people get suspicious?"

Chang nodded his head. "A valid question. What about if we presented ourselves as two eunuchs? As you may have noticed from my friend last night, if one is castrated before puberty, none of the traits associated with being a man develop. I do believe you would have to put on some weight as time went by, though, to perpetuate the image."

Hui filed that one away to think about. "And what about a love life? What if I meet a man and fall in love? I have thought I might like to have children at some point."

"That is something I think we'd have to address if and when the occasion arose. Although I am setting myself up as a merchant, there are still things I am involved in that could be dangerous.

67

Presenting yourself as a eunuch could draw you into my world. Anyone you were to meet would be suspect in my eyes. Given today's political climate, he should be in yours, too."

Our primary focus should be on self-preservation. The options Chang was presenting seemed our only way out. Hui, as one of Wu's ladies-in-waiting, was a wanted woman. Li Xian (or his advisors) would not take kindly to her disappearance – execution was a more reliable form of ensuring compliance with the change in regime. They did not know and probably did not care that Hui had no political aspirations.

I could see no other option for us but "hiding in plain sight." I bemoaned the fact that I could not speak to my human. Projecting images or emotions (or dampening them) was very limiting for someone who was supposed to help their human. However, I tried. An image of Hui dressed as a boy, sitting in a corner, carving her flutes with others surrounding but paying no attention to her. Another of her/him walking down a street, passersby ignoring her. As a boy, she would draw no attention. I did not know enough about eunuchs to "comment" on that part of it.

Hui made up her mind. "I will consent to being a boy – for now. A eunuch? Can we wait on that? Whatever you're involved with outside of the obvious business, I want no part and you know that. How and when do we change me? What about clothing?"

Chang clapped his hands. "Excellent. I believe Gang's clothing will fit you. We will make the change at the rest stop this evening."

At the travel stop, which was nothing more than a hut, while the servants tended the horses and gathered enough wood to start a fire, Chang lengthened Hui's stride. Women were taught to walk quietly by almost gliding with each step. Men, on the other hand, had no such directions. Chang tried to get her to put her weight behind each step. He also taught her to stand more upright than she had, pulling her shoulders back. It would not be an overnight transition, but at least she learned to *think* about her posture and mannerisms.

After they had eaten, Chang cleaned his knife and cut over a foot off Hui's hair. He threw the cuttings onto the fire, which sent up a plume of foul-smelling smoke, causing everyone to cough.

Chang shrugged. "Can't be helped. There are magic users who can trace someone through body parts, including a couple I know on Li Xian's staff. If you are to disappear, you must do it even from them."

Hui pulled part of her hair into a male topknot. Gang handed her an oilskin packet, then he and the other three men left the hut. Unwrapping the package, Hui found a jacket, underskirt, over-robe and a pair of boots. With the exception of the boots, everything was styled very much like what she was already wearing, but plainer and of far inferior fabric. Underneath everything was a leather belt with a pouch and a loop. Women usually kept their personal belongs in a small drawstring purse and their eating dagger in a fold of their robe. She quickly changed, tucked me and my tube into the robe folds, and transferred her things to the belt.

"It's cold out here. Have you changed, yet?" Chang called from outside.

"Yes, you may come back."

The men gathered around the fire to warm themselves but eyed Hui, trying to determine whether she would pass as a boy. Chang finished his appraisal. "I believe you will pass, as long as we continue to work on your acting skills. Now, Hui-the-girl must disappear completely. What is name, boy?"

"My name is Wencheng, kind sir. It is a pleasure to meet you." Hui kept her arms at her side rather than clasp her hands and inclined her head only slightly.

All four men clapped. "Just the right attitude," said Chang. To his servants, "What do you think? Thirteen? Fourteen?"

Hu said, "If he is not to be a eunuch, then he cannot have reached puberty. That generally happens around twelve or thirteen. However, he is too big to be such a child."

No matter how small she might have been, at nearly forty, Hui could not pass for a pre-pubescent male.

"Yes, and there is also the question of his woodcarving talents. He would not be that accomplished at such a young age. I'm afraid, my dear, that we have just run into a problem," Chang addressed Hui. "While you make a fine-looking young man, you look too old to be pre-pubescent."

Hui shrugged. "If I must, I must. You will have to tell me further how I should act, then. What do we do with my old clothing? It paints me as having come from Court, even the casual robes I brought."

"I have contacts in Yangzhou who will be happy to exchange such finery for something a little less so. Now, we must sleep, but keep one eye open. This is not the safest place to be but we had no choice. The others will take turns guarding the horses. Can you ward the hut in such a way that they can come and go but no one else can?"

Hui thought for a moment. "I do not have such skills. I can make the wood impenetrable and seal the door, but I do not know how to allow the others in and out of that ward."

Hu, Da and Gang exchanged a flurry of hand gestures. Hu turned to Chang and Hui. "The night is chilly, but not unreasonably so and it is dry. We can make do with our furs and a fire outside. The two of you are more important and should stay in here behind wards. I will whistle if anything unseemly approaches."

After the others had left, Hui hardened the wood walls of the hut and fused the door to the walls. She and Chang arranged their sleeping furs and bedded down for the night. With nothing else to do, I sang them to sleep, then settled down myself.

Chapter Ten

All five gave thanks to the Universe for keeping them safe from bandits through the night, and after arranging the hut for the next travelers, we started on the final leg of our journey back to Yangzhou. We entered the city as dusk was settling and Hui squinted through the gloaming to see if anything was familiar. We had been gone almost twenty years, and not much was left of the city she remembered.

Gang pulled the coach into the yard of a fairly large house only a few blocks from the wharves. Chang and Hui disembarked, and the other three started taking the trunks off the carriage.

"Welcome home, my dear," Chang said as he ushered her into the house. "Your sleeping room is down the hall to the left. I will have a workshop built adjacent to that room in the next week. Mama! Where are you? We are tired and hungry!"

A wizened little lady appeared from the back of the house. She greeted Chang with a nod of her head, and only gave Hui a passing glance. "Hush. I did not know when to expect you. As soon as I heard the coach I started dinner. It will be a few minutes. Who is the boy?"

Hui had passed her first test. "Mama, this is Wencheng. I brought him with me from Court. He was too valuable to leave within Li Xian's grasp."

She nodded. "I understand. I will set another place at table." Without another word, she turned back in what I assumed was the direction of the kitchen.

"Mama?" Hui queried.

Chang chuckled. "Not my mother, of course. She is actually Da's aunt. I bought her several years ago, after Da told me she was going to be put out on the street because her former owner had died. She's a good cook and housekeeper, and like everyone else I keep

71

around me, knows how to keep her mouth shut. For whatever reason, everyone calls her Mama.

"Go to your room and pull out whatever clothing or other items you do not wish to keep. After we eat, I will send them with Hu to my friend. He will return with more suitable clothing for you."

Another phase of our life had begun. True to his word, Chang had a small workshop attached to Hui's sleeping quarters, which looked out on the back yard. It was small enough that it could be made very comfortable with only a charcoal brazier. Chang also found a supplier of bamboo until the stand he had planted next to the house matured. Hui happily went back to her first passion – making instruments that made beautiful music.

It only took a couple of years for Hui's flutes to become *the* ones to own. Hui was never seen by the public, but the maker's mark she put beneath the embouchure became almost a status symbol for musicians and Yiji alike. It took between one and three months to make a flute (depending on the size and whether it was a *dizi*, a side-blown flute with a vibrating membrane, or a *xaio*, an end-blown flute). Therefore, once Chang established the market, Hui had orders over a year out.

After many turbulent years, up to and including the An Shi Rebellion when many of Chang's acquaintances lost their lives, the Tangs finally regained control of the empire, and life slowly returned to a semblance of normalcy. You may have surmised by now that Hui gave almost no thought to a love life. She found the freedom of being a male quite to her liking and, living in Chang's house with all his secrets, did not feel like testing the waters with her own. That is not to say the members of the household did not know. They did. But Chang was a shrewd enough judge of character to know who would be trustworthy enough to serve him.

Chang, who by this time was getting old, even for a magic practitioner, decided it was time to train a successor. He brought An-Jian into the house. An-Jian was also a eunuch, one whom Chang had met through an associate. Only two years after that, Chang finally passed beyond.

With Chang gone, so were many of Hui's protections. An-Jian was just as politically-involved as Chang, perhaps even more so. However, he was not as circumspect in his dealings – Hui heard comings-and-goings at all hours of the day and night. She knew they were not all legitimate business associates. It was time to move, once again.

Thankfully, due to the prices Hui's flutes commanded, plus the long life, added to which was free living in Chang's house, Hui had amassed quite a bit of money in her years since leaving Court. Chang had taught her how to manage her own finances, which she did. While this was normal for a male, it would have astounded most people had they known otherwise. Therefore, it was not as if she would be dependent on An-Jian for the basic necessities of life.

Xiasheng, Hui's identity assumed during the An Shi Rebellion, leased a small building in the center of Yangzhou – it housed both a workshop and living quarters. With only two servants, one to see customers and the other to keep the house, Xiasheng was considered almost a ghost by the general public. It only heightened the interest in his flutes.

It was a good thing we had moved to our own quarters. Five years after we left, forces of the local military governor descended on An-Jian's household and killed everyone there. It took some time to find out why, but he had been somehow involved in the takeover of the government in Chang'An by eunuchs and was seen as a threat to the local governor.

Hui finished her days as a hermit. She grew obsessed with making the "perfect" flute and would see no one except Bik, the housekeeper. No matter how I tried to redirect her focus to something else, she fixated on one flute. In retrospect, I believe she developed dementia, although at that time, there was no word for such a thing. Finally, in her one hundred seventieth year, her heart gave out, and so did mine.

Chapter Eleven

I left the ether and opened my eyes with a teat in my mouth. I thanked the Universe for putting me in a mammal again. This time there was no sound of children or the comfort of a bed of straw inside a building. Instead, I was curled with my mother and siblings in a nest in the crook of a tree, high off the ground. I had fur, a long snout, an even longer tail, and claws at the ends of my paws that looked like they would be dangerous when I matured. The air was warm and humid, and filled with the sounds of birds and other creatures.

I was what you call a coati, or a coati-mundi. I learned how to climb down the tree after about a month and over the course of the next few months, our mother taught us how to forage for our food by picking fruit off trees, catching lizards as they napped, and digging for insects. Those claws came in handy! My siblings and I played a lot, overseen by not only our mother but others in our pack.

When I matured at about six months of age, I was encouraged to leave the pack and go out on my own. Males were, by nature, solitary, and except for mating, not welcome in the family group. I did not mind. It was time to seek the human with whom I had been paired. I wandered the jungle, eating when I was hungry and sleeping in trees at night, avoiding at all cost other males' territories, always trying to find a human settlement.

It took almost a year, but I finally came close enough to a human settlement to sense their magic. There was a lot of it, and I had to discern that which I knew was *mine*. Therefore, I headed toward trees that were on the edge of cultivated fields where people were at work and waited. I did not have to wait long. A boy, probably about six or eight years of age, passed under the tree where I perched, in search of fallen branches to use as firewood. *This* was my human! I quickly scrambled down the tree and as embarrassing as this is to relate, jumped around like an over-eager dog in an effort to gain his attention. He just laughed at my antics and continued to pick up wood. When his arms were full, he turned toward what I presumed was home. I followed, chittering at him.

He did not return to a house but to a place alongside the field where a blanket had been spread. He, along with other children, dropped their armloads onto the blanket and returned to the trees for more. I continued to follow and chitter. An older woman noticed my activity.

"Tlan," she said. "It seems you have a new friend."

"It has been following me for the last hour," my human answered.

She smiled and peered at my hindquarters, below my tail, which was naturally held high above my back. "If *he* continues to follow you, we will adopt him into the family. *But*, he must stay outside. Junkots can be just as destructive as your friend's monkey."

"Yes, Mama," he answered. I knew *I* would not give in to the baser instincts of my species, but they did not yet know that. Tlanextic was still young, and his magic would not manifest for a few years. I had time to convince them I was different.

I followed him around for the next few hours as he collected more wood. When the blanket was sufficiently full, the mother gathered the corners together, fastened them with a leather cord and swung the bundle over her back, placing a loop in the cord around her forehead. She, Tlanextic, and two other children headed for home.

With me trailing behind, they made their way down what passed for streets, past a large, pyramid-shaped building, three others which were rectangular but spectacularly painted, and numerous others. It was a fairly large city yet felt isolated due to the number of trees.

Home was a hut with three sides of wood posts and the fourth a solid stone wall. These sat on a raised stone base, with a thatched roof that overhung what you would call a porch. The walls were only high enough to preserve privacy – that let in plenty of air. It had only one room. The kitchen was a separate building, approximately five or six feet away from the main house. A second set of buildings matched the first – probably another family's home. There was another building which, I discovered in my explorations, was used to make pottery – two men were hard at work fashioning clay into pots. Centered between the buildings was a garden, growing food for the households. The compound was surrounded by a low stone wall.

I determined the best way to ingratiate myself to the family was to sleep with Tlanextic and prove to them I would not destroy their home. While I waited for night, I dug in the garden for insects to eat, carefully avoiding precious plants.

After the family bedded down for the night on their woven mats, I easily scaled one of the poles holding up the roof support, hopped over to the top of the wall, then down off it into the house. It took no time for me to find Tlan (as he was affectionately known), lie down next to him and lay my tail across his chest. I slept peacefully, knowing I was where I was supposed to be.

The next morning we were awakened to the sound of chuckling. As Tlan and I opened our eyes, the mother's voice said, "I believe this is your *way*, Tlan." (She pronounced it "why.") "He has made it his business to stay close to you. Therefore, you must ensure his health and well-being, as his destiny is entwined with yours. Will you name him?"

Tlan rubbed the sleep from his eyes. "May I think about it?"

"Of course," was the reply. "Come to breakfast. Then you must help Papa today."

I will tell you that Tlan gave me the name, "T'u'ul," which is pronounced "too-ool." He named me after their trickster god because coatis, or junkots as the males are called in their language, are known to be mischievous. I was almost insulted, knowing I would not be like the rest of my species, until I realized I was named after a god. I thought it fitting until I received yet another metaphysical slap, accompanied by, "*Some humility would not go amiss with you.*"

The next few years were spent learning about their culture right along with Tlan. I learned they believed everyone had a *way*, a spirit companion, whose life was intertwined with their own. Only a lucky few saw their *way* manifest into a corporeal body. If that happened, that person was destined for great things, possibly becoming a shaman or priest within their culture. "Tlanextic" was his common name, if you will. It means "strong light" or "light of dawn." His true name was a combination of a god's name and a number, based on the day he was born. This name was used by his parents and the priests during rituals and ceremonies.

He spent most of his days in the pottery building with his father, who told him of their gods and their many calendars while shaping cooking and storage pots, and incense burners. When I was not looking for food, I curled up in a shady spot outside the pottery to listen and learn. It was Tlan's duty to see that the kiln fire was kept at a certain temperature by adding wood to the fire or stirring the coals so the heat was distributed evenly. Twice a week, he and his siblings went with their mother to collect wood for the fires in the kiln and kitchen. As he grew older, he learned to dig clay not far from the shores of the lagoon and river on which they lived, then shape it into the wares his father and uncle sold to merchants, and also traded for the things they did not produce themselves, like maize. The few holidays they had were joyous occasions, celebrating this god or that judicious day, and watching a ball game.

I have given you enough hints. Do you know where I was?

"The calendars are probably the strongest hint, right? If that's the case, my guess is with the Maya at some point."

Very good! Your education is not quite as lacking as I thought.

"I didn't learn that in school. It was all the hype around the winter solstice in 2012 and the end of the world conspiracies."

In that case, I retract my statement. But yes, you are correct. I understand the city is now called Lamanai, which means "sunken crocodile." It is an apt name given the animals that inhabit that area. It sits on a lagoon which is part of a river that drains into the ocean. Therefore, it was an important trading center. But I digress.

At the age of twelve, Tlan had his coming-of-age ceremony, along with others in the city who were determined to be at or past puberty so it was time for them to be considered adults. Almost immediately after the ceremony, Tlan's parents spoke with the parents of a neighbor girl to arrange a marriage. This did not sit well with Tlan. Although the marriage would have been beneficial to both families as they were each well-known potters, he thought the girl shallow and not even very attractive. This should have been my clue, but I was hungry and thinking about where the next meal of beetles, grubs, or lizards might be found rather than paying attention to Tlan's emotions.

Tlan interrupted the parents' conversation with an emphatic, "No!" All four turned to him, aghast that one of their children would dare intrude on the discussion. "My apologies," he continued, "but

I do not wish this marriage. If you force me to go through with it, I will repudiate her immediately."

"Tlanextic," his father began, "the marriage will not happen for several years. You may change your mind in that space of time."

"I *will not!*" He stamped his foot to emphasize his feelings, and we felt the ground tremble. That drew my thoughts away from my stomach, and I quickly tamped his emotions. I would interject a thought here. Although I know your magic generally manifests with strong emotions, why must it be anger? Just one time, I would like for one of my humans to manifest with joy.

"I don't know."

It was a rhetorical question. Back to my tale.

His mother sighed. "It is as I feared so many years ago when the junkot appeared," she said. "He has powerful magic. He will need to study with a shaman. That negates any marriage until he is trained."

The other couple nodded and turned away.

"Tlan," his father said as gently as he could. "You have exhibited strong magic. That is something I cannot teach you to control. I know you are not suited for the priesthood, but I will consult with K'inich anyway about training you."

Tlan opened his mouth to protest. His father held up a hand to forestall any objections. "This is something you cannot argue with. Once K'inich determines you are ready, he will decide your path. But the gods have spoken, and there is no denying the gift you have been given."

And so it was that Tlan and I moved from his parents' home into a building that housed unmarried men. Along with two other young men who had magic (and familiars), they studied by day with the shaman known as K'inich. They were taught some healing – which herbs to use for what and which gods to petition for what; and divination – how to read the skies for portents, and how to read the various calendars. There was also training in their various elemental magics. K'inich was an Air elemental, but he had assistant priests with other affinities. Within just a few days, Tlan had learned enough of his magic and my role that I was accepted. We began to converse, with me projecting images and emotions, Tlan just thinking back to me. K'inich was pleased with our progress, but not so much with Tlan's fellow students. They resisted their destiny and had constant headaches.

For several weeks during the dry season, they, along with other men, took their turns as corvée labor to help build whatever structure the ruler of the time wanted. These men were more conscripts than volunteers but it was considered an honor to assist the king. Sometimes the work was cutting and hauling limestone, others it was fitting the stone together under the direction of the stone workers, or masons as you call them today. At night, despite their exhaustion, K'inich would grill them on what they felt or discovered while laboring.

Tlan learned he had an affinity for the stone. He instinctively knew which in the quarry area was the most hardened, making it best for buildings. The somewhat softer material was for the artists who carved statues and stelae – also at the behest of the ruler; or small statuettes for personal use sold in the market.

Three years into his studies, K'inich announced that Tlan was not suitable for the life of a shaman, confirming his father's original assessment. Although he learned his lessons well, he had no true aptitude for healing or divination. Tlan's apprenticeship was passed to Nu'un, a stone mason. Nu'un had a familiar, an ocelot.

Nu'un taught Tlan how to pulverize the stone, heat it, and add water in just the right amount for the cement that held the building blocks together. Another mixture proportion was just perfect as plaster to coat the buildings in preparation for painting. More lessons were about proper application of the cement or plaster. A trickle of magic moved a stone block a half inch to perfectly align it. Another trickle and the plaster was as smooth as the proverbial baby's bottom. It was not as easy a life as it sounds. Not only did they build, they also quarried. Magic only helped so far in that regard. The stone still had to be chiseled out of the ground with obsidian tools, raised to the surface by pulleys, hauled to the building site using logs as rollers, and if they were working on a tall structure, raised into position by yet more pulleys. The stone wall of a house was easier – the blocks were smaller and the walls not so high, so the building could progress with fewer hands.

To forestall your question, Tlan tried *one* time to raise a stone with magic. You are an Earth elemental as well, so please imagine the effort it would take to raise a block of stone weighing thirty tons or more. Even with my help, he did not succeed in elevating it a full inch before we both collapsed. It took us nearly three days to recover from that one effort, and another day to recover from the tongue-lashing Nu'un gave us. After Tlan was appropriately contrite, Nu'un chuckled and told him every Earth stone worker had tried it at least once, and Tlan was lucky he collapsed when he did – one of Nu'un apprentices a few decades earlier had died from his efforts.

When Nu'un caught Tlan using magic to etch faces into the stone he was supposed to be setting (and as quickly covering his work with cement or plaster), it became clear his path lay in yet another direction. Tlan's apprenticeship was transferred again, this time to a sculptor named Waxa. Tlan was first tasked to claim the best carving stone for his master. This was not quite as easy as it might seem. Waxa, while popular, was not the only sculptor wanting to lay claim to the best pieces coming from the quarry. But Tlan had the advantage of being able to read the stone and passed on many pieces crowed over by other apprentices with the same charge.

The quarrying took place during the dry season. Once the rains arrived, it was time for Tlan to learn the fine art of sculpting. As a yet unmarried man, Tlan moved from the bachelors' quarters into Waxa's household. We were given a corner of a house behind the workshop. The workshop had no walls – simply posts sunk into the stone floor to hold the thatched roof. The reason it had no walls was to let in as much light as possible. The downside to not having walls was when the winds blew the rain, the blocks got wet. You may remember from your studies with Gregory that limestone is very soft and will erode, although slowly according to human time. Waxa had devised a clever cover for anything he was working on – several leaves from a banana tree sewn together to make a waterproof drape of sorts. Underneath the roof were blocks large enough to create a stela; other, smaller ones would be used for statues and statuettes.

Waxa did not have magic. What he *did* have was the current king's favor, which explained the blocks for stelae. Only a king could commission a stela, although some of the more prosperous members of court and merchants might commission a smaller one as a tombstone for a family member. Tlan learned that one did not simply start to work on a piece of stone for an important stela. Before a single stroke of a chisel hit the stone, priests were consulted. First and foremost, for the most auspicious day to begin work. Then, which hieroglyphics should be carved, based on the information the buyer wanted to convey. It could be something having to do with their gods, an announcement of sorts of a victory over a rival tribe, accomplishments of the person being lauded by the stela, almost anything. A sketch of one or more sides of the block was provided to the buyer for his approval, and once that was obtained, actual work began - on the day the priests deemed the best.

While waiting for an approval or the start-day, Waxa carved smaller statues of their gods. These took perhaps a half-day each to complete and allowed Waxa a steady stream of income between large commissions. I found it interesting that while his statues looked almost identical to those carved by other sculptors and sold either at the market or to exporters, Waxa's commanded a higher price due to his current favor with the king. He had no need of a stall at the market, either. People came to his workshop where an assistant handled the transactions while Waxa, oblivious to the commerce going on around him, chipped away at stone.

Tlan's other duty as Waxa's apprentice was to sweep the floor. Unsurprisingly, a lot of stone chunks fell away while carving, and it was up to Tlan to ensure the floor beneath Waxa's feet was always clean – stepping on one of those chunks was not only painful, it could cause a loss of balance during a delicate stroke, ruining whatever Waxa was working on. That allowed Tlan to watch what Waxa was doing. But that only lasted a month or so, until Waxa was able to get a slave from the most recent skirmish.

Slave? Skirmish?

Of course. Just like almost any other society from the beginning of time, the Maya fought against their neighbors for land, ego, whatever motivates you humans to fight. The enemies they did not kill, or who did not flee, were captured and made slaves. Some were kept for ballgames played on holidays. Others were sold to generate income for the king.

So, once the slave was obtained, Tlan graduated to learning to chisel the stone. He started on smaller pieces – larger chunks that had been carved off the most recent stela and re-smoothed into a block. His first attempt was an unmitigated disaster. It looked *nothing* like the statuette Waxa had provided as a guideline. Tlan attempted to correct his errors with magic, only to discover he could not add stone back in where it had been removed.

"This is why I give you cast-offs to practice on," Waxa said with a smile. "I know you can just as easily remove stone with your magic as you can a chisel, but you need to know *what* to remove before you start. You must *see* the finished product in your mind and free that image from the block."

81

That was easier said than done for the novice. Even with his magic, he took *weeks* to learn to carve the stone so it bore some resemblance to what it was supposed to be. The only advantage he had over Waxa was being able to do the finer carving and smoothing with his magic, rather than a smaller chisel or a piece of pumice.

Tlan carved for four hours each day and spent the rest of the day helping Waxa's assistant. The assistant, Xin, was tasked with not only selling the statuettes but trading or exchanging some of the payment into goods, whether stone for work, clothing, or food for the house. Xin's wife, Sacniete performed all housekeeping duties. They lived in another house behind the workshop, so she cooked for everyone in the shared kitchen then, after cleaning up the final meal of the day, she and Xin retired to their own home.

Tlan grew up with their ballgame as a recreational sport, although he did not want to participate in the professional games which were played by local soldiers against captured soldiers and the losers decapitated. He and a few apprentices of his acquaintance played a smaller version in one of the common areas. Until, that is, Tlan cheated and was caught. You see, the ball they played with was made of rubber, which at that time was a natural substance, yes? Tlan discovered he could control the direction of the ball, and it was easy to prevent the ball from hitting the ground, which it was not supposed to do. One rare afternoon off, the boys were playing their game and a witch walked by. She saw the flows of Tlan's magic, and called him on it. He was literally dragged by his ear to Waxa and the charge presented.

Cheating, then as now, was an offense against the gods – and masters. It was within Waxa's right to have Tlan put to death for bringing shame on his boss. Waxa held off on the ultimate sentence and instead, demoted Tlan back to the slave's position. The slave was sold to a neighbor, and Tlan was back to sweeping the floor, hauling water from the lagoon, and anything else menial anyone in the household could think of. The only time he was excused from his duties were public holidays. When he was not being watched, Tlan managed some of his work, especially the sweeping, with magic, but most of the time, it was physical. I had little to do during this time and am ashamed to say, I overate and gained a lot of weight.

It took almost a year before Waxa determined Tlan had learned his lesson, bought another slave, and re-introduced Tlan to sculpting.

Again, it took a long time for Tlan to be able to carve a statue to Waxa's satisfaction. Once he had the basics down, Waxa allowed him to add his own touches…a slight change in clothing here, an additional feather or other ornamentation there. These Xi sold to a local artist, who painted them before selling them in his market stall.

Chapter Twelve

About ten years into Tlan's apprenticeship, Waxa received a *huge* commission: he was to decorate the doorway to the king's new home. All other work was set aside while the planning took place. The painter who would color Waxa's carving was brought in to consult on the best carving depth to better show off the colors. Tlan was tasked to Xi full-time, but there were enough lulls in activity that he could watch Waxa and Aj, the painter. Mostly Aj. Tlan thought Aj a fine specimen of a man and quickly fell in lust. As an apprentice, Tlan should have been below Aj's notice, but it seemed Tlan's feelings were reciprocated, because even after he and Waxa had completed their plans, Aj found reasons to come back to the stone sculptor's workshop...at first for statuettes to color while waiting for the big project to begin, then finally asking Waxa's permission to speak directly to Tlan. This occurred after the doorway had been completed and life in the workshop had returned to normal.

And so began the courtship of Aj and Tlan. Aj was four years older than Tlan, a Water wizard, and came from a family of painters, most of whom were also Water wizards or witches. Some did murals, others the fine work of painting ceramics. Two uncles specialized in making paints which were used by family members or sold to other artists. Aj was the only one living who painted statuettes and at the same time, made his own paints. They, all twenty or so including family members and a couple of slaves, lived in a huge compound outside the city center, along the river and very close to the city's port and trading center. As a full-fledged artist in his own right, Aj was Tlan's better in society, but they both knew there would come a time when Tlan would be released from Waxa's custody and go out on his own. At that point, they would be equals. They made plans to be together both in their personal and business lives.

Three years after the doorway commission, Waxa finally determined he could teach Tlan no more and released him into the world. Aj and Tlan were married according to Maya custom and

Tlan moved into Aj's household and workshop. The biggest disagreement I can remember them having was very early on, when the dust from Tlan's carving floated its way into the paints Aj was making. The dust was finer than the ground seashells being used to make a purple paint and could not be strained out. The argument was so heated, I had to put a clamp on Tlan's temper – I was afraid he would cause something to erupt. Something did explode, but it was not because of Tlan. Remember, Aj was a Water wizard. That purple paint he was making by soaking a particular kind of seashell in water sprayed all over everything and everyone. *That* diffused the tempers as both men dissolved into laughter, pointing at all the purple splotches on each other.

The issue was resolved by adding a small area onto the back of Aj's workshop, with a curtain of banana leaves between. Those were thick enough that the stone dust didn't penetrate into Aj's work area. It was a very harmonious working relationship. The aunts tasked with selling the family's wares let them know what was in demand, both locally and what the traders in the port wanted, and they made their statues according to that information.

Tlan was about one hundred years old when the uncles who made paint passed beyond. Both were relatively young for wizards and neither had thought to train a new generation. The family met and agreed that Aj would make paint full-time as well as train whichever nieces or nephews showed interest. Tlan didn't want anyone painting his statues other than Aj, and after some discussion, it was agreed the two men would make the paint together. Tlan's Earth affinity would determine which clay was to be dug to thicken the colors, as well as helping to properly mix it.

I relished this period in his life. As we walked the riverbank, looking for good clay deposits, I was able to run in the forest and just be a coati. I even played with some of Aj's grand-nieces and -nephews because everyone knew a familiar would not harm the children. As the only familiar in the family, I was treated with great respect. Of course, I helped Tlan when it was required, but it was an easy time.

After about twenty years of making paint full-time, Aj became sick as his uncles had. He had difficulty breathing, weakened dramatically, and eventually became bedridden. A healer was called in and determined Aj's lungs were clogged. As with the uncles, Air wizards tried to pull the blockage from his lungs – probably a buildup of mucus from inhaling the ground substances they used to make the paints – to no avail. They did all they could, but Aj passed just as his uncles had.

Tlan was heartbroken. It took everything I had to convince him not to suicide and put himself into the care of their goddess Ixtab. The family was a great help in this regard, as well. At least one family member was with Tlan at all times; one grand-nephew slept in the corner of Tlan's sleeping hut each night. Slowly but surely, he was convinced to go back to work at his first love, carving. Rather than use stone which, to him, brought back too many memories, Tlan started working with wood. His predecessor had taught me a lot about working with bamboo, so I was able to show him how to carve around flaws, or smooth them out, as was required for whatever he was working on. The benefit of working with wood was any discards could simply be used in cooking fires.

After about a year, Tlan thought his work could finally be brought to the public. The nieces who had taken over marketing and selling from the aunts created a demand for his boxes in the shape of temples, or square boxes with a hieroglyphic blessing carved into them. The rest of the family privately sighed with relief – Tlan would be contributing to his own upkeep once again. He was out of the woods as far as suicide went, but he was still a very sad man.

Tlan finally found joy again when he started carving animal figurines. Unlike the stone statuettes which were, in today's eyes, stylized, these were very lifelike. He used his magic to ensure that the eyes looked alive, the fur or feathers almost soft enough to stroke. They were not sold. They were first given to all the little ones living in the family compound. Then, he started carrying a sack of them when he walked through the city for one reason or another. Every child he met was gifted a carving from that bag. The smiles lighting the children's faces were enough to lift him out of his depression.

When Tlan started to age and no longer took his walks through the city, one of the priests started bringing children to the compound to be gifted one of Tlan's animals. It became almost a rite of passage for the younger ones...they would walk hand-in-hand with the priest, eyes downcast, and nerves would be in evidence as Tlan held out the sack for them to pick one blindly. After they saw what they had picked out, the nerves disappeared, and they raised their eyes to

Tlan with joy. I think that was what kept him going long after most wizards would have passed beyond.

But time takes its toll for everyone. At the ripe old age of three hundred fifty-two, Tlan took his last breath sitting outside his hut, carving. The last I saw before I vanished into the ether was his hands drooping, dropping his knife and the piece of wood he had been working on.

Chapter Thirteen

If my previous life was the most serene, the next was perhaps the most tumultuous.

I was relieved to find myself once again a mammal. (I hoped and continue to hope I am never an insect again.) This time, I woke as a puppy nursing on his mother. As I grew and started exploring with my brothers and sisters, I discovered I was on a farm of sorts where the buildings were surrounded by lemon trees which, in turn, were looked down on by mountains. From the house, I could see ocean.

The house was the home of a family headed by a witch who was known throughout the region for her healing potions. Her familiar, Luca, was the same breed dog as I was, albeit quite a bit older and from another mother. She had a large herb garden where she grew what she needed for healing. Her son, a wizard, managed the lemon orchards. His wife, who had no magic, kept house, tended the kitchen garden, and supervised their six children. When I was about three months of age, the old lady came to where we were nested in a corner of a barn, surveyed the litter and with a smile, plucked me from the pile. She carried me to the house and handed me to a young man. "He will be your lifelong friend," she told him. "Take care of him, and he will take care of you." I was named, "Arsenio," which, in their language means strong and virile. It was a fitting name. I was what you would call a Cane Corso, a large breed used then for protection and tracking. When we were both adults, my head was nearly to my human's hip.

He was named Uberto, and at that time, he was about ten years old and the youngest boy. Even at that age, he showed an aptitude for making potions, which meant rather than helping in the orchards along with his older brothers, he learned by watching his grandmother. Of course, that was thought to be women's work, and he was teased about it by his siblings, but that did not seem to worry him much. He and I learned about herbs while she was working in the garden, how and which herbs to mix into wine for which ailment, and how to deal with clients when they visited. This last was accomplished by sitting quietly just outside the door when the grandmother consulted.

I believe I must explain a few things at this point. We were on what is now known as the Amalfi Coast of Italy. At that time, it was either part of the Kingdom of Naples or the Kingdom of Sicily, depending on which political faction was in power at the time, but under Spanish rule. If you will recall your history, that part of the world, almost without exception, followed the Catholic faith, and my human and his family did, as well. Of course, they used their magic, and none of the locals blinked an eye, but they prayed to their god several times each day and attended church every Sunday and every holy day, as well. I sat quietly whenever Uberto did his praying, trotted alongside him on the way to the ancient cathedral, and waited outside until they were done.

When Uberto was about twelve, he was working in his grandmother's stillroom, attempting to make a drink for a local noble's rheumatism, when his grandmother yelled at him for not paying attention to the herbs he was using. He had grabbed the mandrake root rather than astragalus, and she was right to stop him before he accidentally poisoned the man. He lost his temper, angry with himself, and the clay pots she used for storage flew off the shelf. Thankfully, Angelina was a strong witch with a little Air ability to complement her Earth and was able to stop the jars' flight and return them to their shelves before anything broke. Uberto, who had grown up watching his grandmother's, father's, and older siblings' magic, gaped at her. She chuckled.

"I see your magic has decided to manifest at last," she told him. "I was beginning to worry. *Now* I can start teaching you the real healing."

She looked from Uberto to me and back again. "Remember when I gave Arsenio to you and told you he would be your lifelong friend?" Uberto nodded. "He is your familiar, just as Luca here is mine. If you protect him as well as he will protect you, he will be with you for your long life. You will feel pressure at the back of your brain, like the start of a headache. Do not reach for the willow bark.

That is Arsenio. If you accept him and his help, that headache will never materialize. Do you understand?" Uberto nodded again.

Because he had grown up around magic *and* someone who had a familiar, there was no painful transition from child and pet to wizard and familiar. He continued on with the potion he was making, with Angelina showing him how to inject energy into the drink when it had finished brewing. Over the next several months, she showed him how to help plants which were struggling, and how to inject different kinds of energy into different kinds of herbal preparations.

The noble who benefitted from Uberto's rheumatism drink continued to come around even when he needed nothing, simply observing Uberto at work. It made my human nervous, but since there was nothing he could do about it, he made every effort to ignore the great man. Within a few months, with Angelina's permission, he spoke to Uberto about proper schooling.

"I see great potential in you," the man known to us as Don Marco began in their native Neapolitan language. "Your grandmother has already taught you a lot about medicine, and I know you have *some* Latin, at least enough to say the Paternoster and a few other things. I would like to send you to the school at Salerno to learn how to speak, read, and write Latin fluently, and more about medicine than your grandmother can teach you. When you graduated, you would become part of my retinue as my doctor. Would that be of interest to you?"

Uberto, who was no fool, asked if he could think about it and was granted until the next day to make up his mind. After Don Marco departed, he turned to his grandmother. "The schooling interests me, of course. But to become one of his retainers? I do not wish to become embroiled in court politics. What do you think?"

Angelina frowned. "It is a risk, I agree. And although Salerno is no longer as prestigious as it once was, the reward would still be worth it. Although he was somewhat incorrect. I can teach you as much about medicine as any Don at that school, but I cannot give you the stature that would come with a diploma. Don Marco is not a young man, and you would not have to stay with him for many years. The diploma from Salerno would open many more doors after he is gone to God."

I interjected my thoughts into the conversation, projecting an image of him living in a small room, then me waiting outside on the steps of a building. Uberto looked at me, then back to Angelina. "And what of Arsenio? I could not bear to leave him here, yet I cannot take him to school. He would not be welcome there any more than he is in church."

She nodded, knowing the bond between familiar and human. "If you decide to accept the Don's offer, it must come with the condition that Arsenio be allowed to live with you. He can amuse himself while you are at school, I am sure (she winked at me), yet you would be together all other times."

Uberto spent a sleepless night (and because his thoughts were in such turmoil, so did I) turning various scenarios around in his head. I tried to calm him, to no avail. When the sun rose, so did we, no matter how bleary-eyed. Angelina, noting the outward signs of no sleep, put him to grinding herbs, which required no real thought. Don Marco arrived at the stillroom when the sun was nearly at its zenith, asking for Uberto's decision. Angelina stood to one side, watching with interest. She had no idea what would happen.

"I am interested, of course, and both flattered and grateful for your offer," Uberto began. "But I have concerns. First, my dog. I do not wish to be parted from him. Second, my length of service to repay you for your kindness. Third, and very important, I have no wish to be involved in politics, and I know by necessity you are."

Don Marco nodded. "You are wise beyond your years, I think. Many do not consider these things, rushing headlong into what seems to be a golden opportunity.

"I have done my calculations, and let us see if you agree with them. The cost of your tuition plus living expenses for the eight years it would take for you to achieve the status of dottore is approximately equal to what a good dottore would earn over ten years. So, you would be in my service for ten years after graduation. Any more than that would be up to you, and we would discuss payment at that point. I will put a provision in my will that should I go to God before you graduate, my heir will continue to pay until you do and you will be a free man at graduation. I will also add, should I go to God before those ten years of service are complete, you will be free upon my death.

"As my dottore, you would, naturally, be required to travel with me between my various houses. But I see no need for you to attend me when I am at court. That would, hopefully, keep you out of the politics. I cannot guarantee that, however. It would be up to you to project an air of complete neutrality, yes?

"And as for your dog. I may have no magic, but I am not ignorant of your ways. Why do you think I have used your grandmother's potions all these years? When at school, you will be staying at my townhouse in Salerno, and your familiar will be welcome to stay with you. I will say, the staff there does not like magic and are very superstitious, so you must not show any outward signs.

"If all this is agreeable with you, we will leave for Salerno in a fortnight's time. I will take you there in my coach, get you settled in the house, and introduce you to Signore Dottore Modrone, who runs the school, before returning here. So, what have you decided?"

Uberto was quiet. Angelina, too, was quiet, although Luca told me she was nervous about Uberto's decision. She really wanted him to take advantage of the opportunity but also understood why he might not. I could tell Uberto was still envisioning as many scenarios as he could. I gave him a mental nudge.

He sighed. "Don Marco. Sir. One last question. What if I either don't like the school or don't do well?"

At this, Don Marco chuckled, then his face took on a serious expression. "I believe you will excel at school. Otherwise, I would not have made the offer in the first place. *But*, if you take my offer, you must stay at school for the full eight years and apply yourself. I will get regular reports on your progress which, by the way, I will share with your grandmother, and if I see any slacking or if any of the masters complain of your behavior, you will be reduced to servant status, and that will be for the rest of my life, plus that of my heir. I also have no doubt your grandmother will mete out punishment in her own unique way."

Angelina was known for her punishments. All of the grandchildren and, I presume, her children when they were younger, knew about her ordering you to, oh, plant a new row of lemon trees with only your bare hands. She would monitor to ensure no magic was used. It was not a pleasant experience, and she generally only had to do it once. The young ones in her family were known for their good behavior. What she could do from a distance and while Uberto was in the Don's household I did not know, but would not put anything beyond her reach.

Uberto went deeper into thought. I nudged him again – this time by butting him with my head, and at this point in his life, I could nuzzle his waist without stretching in the least. He staggered a bit, and Don Marco snickered. "I believe your dog is asking for a decision. As am I."

Uberto sighed again. "It is a big step, but I will accept your offer. You say we leave in a fortnight?"

Angelina blew out the breath she had been holding. Don Marco smiled and held out his hand to Uberto. "At first light, yes. I and my coach will be at your door, waiting. I believe you have made the right decision. Until then?" He shook Uberto's hand, made a slight bow to Angelina and left.

Angelina hugged Uberto. "I, too, believe you have made the right decision. You will be a great dottore. I cannot teach you the other things you might learn, but now we must change your focus from making herbal remedies to what dottores do when they treat patients. It is not the same as being able to observe their body and their aura to determine what is wrong, and I do not want you to make the mistake of correcting your mundane teachers."

Whenever Angelina had a spare moment over the next two weeks, we learned about Galenic and Hippocratic medicine. This was mostly about the four humours, how to discern what was out of balance, and what was generally prescribed to re-balance the body. It was definitely a far cry from how Angelina diagnosed and treated. But that was how mundane professionals worked, and Uberto needed to know that.

"Once you have your diploma, you can use your magic surreptitiously to help a patient. But you must never outwardly deviate from what is taught. That sort of medicine is too well known to anyone who can afford to pay a dottore, and you do not want to run afoul of the law *or* the church, do you understand?" Angelina was getting in some last-minute instruction as Uberto packed his meager belongings in the wee hours of our departure morning.

Uberto groaned, exasperated. "Yes, nonna, I do understand. You have drilled me for two straight weeks on how to present myself in a mundane world. I will not forget!"

About an hour later, Uberto was inside the coach with the Don, and I trotted alongside the two horses pulling it. I was a little surprised when one spoke to me. I had never heard of a familiar as a horse. We had a pleasant conversation (her human was Don

Marco's Master of the Horse) and I learned how she coped with not always being in her human's immediate vicinity. She taught me how to access my human's mind from miles away. It was an informative full day of travel, with a stop at an inn for the humans to eat lunch and those of us with four legs to rest.

We arrived at Don Marco's townhouse as the sun was setting. As they walked into the house, the staff was lined up, headed by the steward, to greet their master. Uberto was introduced, then shown to a room on the third floor by a boy younger than him. While small, it was still larger than the room he shared with his brothers at home. Dinner was a quiet affair. As I ate the meat put down for me by the cook in the kitchen, I listened in on the conversation going on in the dining room.

"These are the rules you will follow for the next eight years," Don Marco began. "First, you will eat with me when I am in the city, but when I am not, you will eat with the servants. You will have no special privileges. Second, when I am not here, you will write me every week, telling me what you have learned and how you are getting along in school. I will compare what you say with the reports I get from Signore Dottore Modrone, and if there is deviation, I will know why."

Uberto interrupted. "Don Marco, I do not know how to write."

"That is something you will learn in school, and you will learn quickly, do you understand? Third, during the day when you are at school, your dog must stay in the stables. He would be underfoot in the house. Since he will be outside, you will ensure he is clean before he re-enters the house. Whether it's just wiping him down or giving him a full bath will be up to Andreas, my steward.

"Tomorrow morning I will take you to the school. After that I must leave on business. You will note the route the coach takes so you can find your way back to the house. When you return from school, Andreas will have you measured for proper clothing. Until that is delivered later this week, one of the houseboys has taken one of his outfits to your room. You are close in size, and something slightly ill-fitting is better than looking like a farmer. Now, do you have any questions?"

"Not at the moment, sir," Uberto replied. "I am sure after tomorrow I will have many. To whom should I address them?"

"Andreas. He is my nephew and as such, has had schooling. He should be able to answer any question you may have, and if not, would know where to get the answer."

Uberto nodded, then yawned. "May I be excused, sir? I think I should try to get some sleep before tomorrow."

"Of course. We will leave after morning prayers."

As promised, the Don took Uberto to school the next morning. I was shooed out of the house to the stables, but thanks to Don Marco's horse, I now knew how to be in my human's head when we were far apart. I found a comfortable spot in the sun and lay down to listen.

Chapter Fourteen

I will not dwell long on those eight years of schooling. Uberto learned to speak, read and write not only Latin but Greek, both of which were necessary not only to study their medical texts, but were considered the mark of an educated man. This he enjoyed, and once he could read, spent his few spare hours in the Don's study, reading nearly every book there. The rest he did not enjoy. Long before they got to any study of medicine, there were weeks upon months of logic and rhetoric. Once he finally moved on to the actual study of medicine, he found what he had learned from his grandmother was sometimes in direct contradiction to what he was being taught. He knew better than to argue, but longed for the days of Angelina's garden and stillroom. His most uncomfortable moment, I believe, was when they dissected a human cadaver. He was not squeamish, nor did he faint as did many of his fellow students, but he felt extremely sorry for the fellow on the table. He knew he would not be making surgery his specialty.

Following his eight years in school, he was required to spend one year as an apprentice to a full doctor. This Don Marco arranged with a friend. We moved from the Don's house to the doctor's, still within the city of Salerno, and Uberto spent his days by the doctor's side, learning first-hand how to treat patients. Here, his herbal knowledge finally came into play. He was more knowledgeable than Dottore Rossi and was better able to instruct the apothecary what was needed to treat ailments. Dottore Rossi, initially not pleased that his apprentice had upstaged him, finally, grudgingly, gave him the respect he was due.

After that year, he underwent a rigorous oral examination back at the school and at last was rewarded with the title of *medicus*, or in the vernacular, dottore.

It was now time to repay Don Marco for his sponsorship. We moved back to the Don's house in Salerno but never spent much time there. Don Marco, now an old man, preferred to spend as much time as possible at his house in Amalfi, leaving business and most of the political maneuvering to his oldest son. We did make one trip to Naples, the capital, where Uberto heard enough to know he would never make a politician.

Living back in Amalfi was soothing to Uberto's soul. He had missed the rugged coast but most especially, his grandmother. She gave him full access to her garden and stillroom, and it was here he made his remedies for the Don's various ailments. When the Don napped in the afternoon, we were able to spend more time with Angelina, learning even more how to *really* treat the sick and injured.

Just four short years after Uberto obtained his degree, Don Marco passed away, and although Uberto was technically released from service, the new Don, Paolo, asked him to stay on as the household doctor. Since we had no other ideas, Uberto accepted. It was a fairly easy life, and being employed by a noble meant decent wages in addition to a roof over our heads and good food – something not always available to the common man.

Our easy life did not last long. Over the years, we naturally had heard of the Inquisition. Then, the King and Queen of Spain (to simplify geography and titles), who ruled over our area, set up their own state-sponsored inquisition to ensure their country and all their possessions stayed Catholic. That did not affect us, however. Uberto and his family were good Catholics, and although it was known in the community they were magic practitioners, they only used it for good. But Uberto had a crisis of conscience when the Inquisition came closer to home and started trying Jews and Muslims who refused to convert to Catholicism. He had been taught *all* life is sacred, which it is, and to see people he knew suffer because they believed differently went against everything he felt. He did not stop believing in their god, but only the way their priests *instructed* they should.

He did not, however, stop praying or going to church. Don Paolo was as cognizant of Uberto's magic as his father had been, but there were some in the household who were wary of magic and it was only by pretending to practice the Catholic faith that Uberto stayed in their good graces. Had he not, one or more would certainly have reported him to the inquisitors as apostate.

The worst was yet to come. As so often happens, despite her ministrations, one of Angelina's patients died, and his family accused her of killing him using magic. This brought the inquisitors to the family's doorstep. Since Luca, as a normal dog, should have long since died, many others came out against her, presumably to save their own skins. Angelina, using Luca and me as messengers, told Uberto to flee – the inquisitors were looking at the entire family.

Before Uberto could say anything, Don Paolo came to our room. Naturally, he had heard of Angelina's plight. "You must leave the country. Now," he told Uberto. "I cannot save your grandmother, nor you if they should come here."

Uberto knew this, but where to go? Don Paolo had already thought of that.

"I have a friend in England who I know will take you in, at least temporarily. I have written a letter of introduction. There is a ship, the *Angelina*, strangely enough, leaving for London on tomorrow morning's tide, and I have booked passage for you and Arsenio. I think it would be best if you boarded the ship as soon as you have packed. I do not know how long it will take them to get here, but the sooner you're gone, the safer you will be. I am sorry, but that is the best I can do without endangering myself."

Uberto thanked him profusely, tucking the letter into his tunic. After Don Paolo left, Uberto hurriedly threw his few belongings, including one precious copy of a medical treatise, into his travel bag. His carefully hoarded ducats went into a pouch tied around his waist and tucked into the top of his stockings underneath his tunic. He threw on his robe and hat, grabbed his bag and after looking to ensure none of the other servants saw us, we quietly left the house and made our way to the port.

We were a day out from Amalfi when Luca told me they were taking Angelina to be hanged. He bid me farewell and asked me to pass on Angelina's love for Uberto. Then he disappeared from my mind. Although I still could not use words with my human, relaying these messages was not difficult. Uberto, naturally, was heartbroken and spent most of the two weeks of travel sitting on the deck, staring out at the vast ocean, thinking of all the time he had spent with his grandmother. In rare moments, he wondered what his new life would be like.

It was a rainy spring day when we arrived at the port of London. The captain, knowing our destination, gave Uberto directions to the house of Signore Cavalcanti, then almost pushed us off his ship – he was anxious to unload his cargo and get paid. We, naturally, got lost within minutes. London was so much larger than any city we had been to before, and street names were not posted anywhere. Not speaking a word of the local language, it was hours before we came across a richly dressed man exiting a carriage that Uberto found someone who spoke Latin.

The man was kind, and although he did not know Signore Cavalcanti, he was familiar with the area he lived in, and gave us directions there. We were told to go to a certain house where Latin would be spoken for further instruction. He gave Uberto a slight bow and continued on his way.

It took us another hour of walking to come to the area known as Austin Friars which, had we but known it, was only an hour's walk from where we disembarked. If we had only turned left instead of right! I had been sneezing almost since arriving on dry land – the unfamiliar smells were bothering me. As were my paws. And Uberto's feet. It was nearly sunset when we finally found the house we had been directed to. After some sign language machinations, the steward made a 'stay' motion with his hands and closed the door in our faces. A few moments later, a portly man came to the door and, in perfect Latin, asked what Uberto wanted. We got our directions, and the door was once again closed in our faces.

It was only about a ten-minute walk around a great church and its surrounding property, but to our sore feet, it felt a lot longer. When we finally arrived at our destination, Uberto thought to me, "I am tired, hungry and sore. If this does not work, you and I will have to sleep on a bench or under a tree somewhere. I cannot go farther."

Uberto knocked on the door and we waited. Again, a steward obviously wanted to know why Uberto was there, but this time, Uberto had the letter addressed to the master of the house (somewhat soggy but the address was still legible) which he wordlessly handed over, assuming there would be a communication problem again. The steward, giving me a gimlet eye, first indicated we should wipe the mud off our feet, then that we should follow him. We were ushered into a parlor where Uberto promptly dropped his bag and sat in the softest-looking chair, not thinking that he was soaked through by rain and would probably do some harm to the upholstery. I gratefully stretched out on the floor next to him. A few minutes later, the door opened, meaning Uberto had to get to his feet. He did so with a groan, then smiled as his host addressed him in Italian, which Uberto had learned in school and which was close in syntax to his native Neapolitan.

"Don Paolo told me of your problems in his letter which, by the way, I have burned to prevent others knowing. Such a sad state of affairs at home, no? You are welcome to stay here until you find your way here in England," Signore Cavalcanti told us and with a wink continued, "Your dog is nothing more than a beloved pet, yes? While here, you *must* learn the English language well enough to get by in the city. My staff all speak it, some better than others. I will instruct them to help you learn. Now, I am certain you are exhausted after your trip. We have already eaten supper, but Alberto will show you to a guest room and I will have Cook send something up for both of you to eat. When you have changed your clothes, give them to Alberto to see to.

"Join me for breakfast in the morning, and we will together figure out something for you to do. I am sure I can make needed introductions, I just have to know *who* to introduce you to!"

The Signore had no idea just how exhausted we were. Uberto, out of pride, did not tell him of our wanderings but instead, simply thanked him. Alberto returned, picked up Uberto's bag and told us to follow him. We did, up the stairs and down a corridor to what, to us, was a palatial room. It was about twice the size of our room in Amalfi, and the bed had not one but three feather mattresses! Uberto stripped out of his wet clothing, changed into a night rail then, after handing his soggy garments to Alberto, dug into the bread, cheese and wine brought up for him. A large piece of game was on a separate platter for me. It did not take long for us to consume every last bit of food then drop into a deep sleep. I woke when Alberto brought the clothes back early the next morning, but as he posed no threat, I let Uberto sleep.

Breakfast was an interesting affair. After morning prayers, which the whole house attended, Uberto was invited to sit with Signore Cavalcanti in the dining room. All servants but Alberto were dismissed, and over another meal of bread and cheese, questions flew back and forth between Uberto and his host.

We found that Signore Cavalcanti was a Florentine. Although firmly Catholic (he had been a gentleman usher to Pope Leo X), he had no problem with witches or wizards who used their magic for good works. He had moved to London about ten years previously to be the English branch of a trade and banking firm, which explained how he and Don Paolo knew each other. He did not have diplomatic status *per se* but was often found at Court, due to his ability to arrange purchase and transport of artwork from all parts of Europe to England…specifically to the various palaces owned by the Crown. Due to his extensive trade and banking connections, he was called on frequently to consult with the Privy Council regarding economic conditions within the various states on the Italian peninsula.

In return, Signore Cavalcanti learned of Uberto's medical training. He was, I am sure, about to suggest various nobles who could use a doctor in the household when Uberto told him he preferred the occupation of apothecary.

"But you are trained at Salerno!" Signore Cavalcanti exclaimed. "Why would you not practice that profession? It would earn you a lot of money here, where so very few graduate from such prestigious schools."

"But I do not wish to practice medicine that way," Uberto began. "I did it for nearly twenty years after graduation and found it to be extremely dissatisfying. In many ways, it went directly contrary to the things my grandmother taught me in her stillroom. If I must start a new life, I would prefer to work with the medicines, not the patients."

"Ah. I had forgotten about your magic, and that presents a problem. Here in the city, you might start a business and have no issues because it's large and the population is varied. However, there are a lot of nobles, and if you anger one, it might bring the authorities to your door more quickly. Conversely, in a smaller town, there is generally only one noble to worry about, but they generally do not like foreigners and by foreigners, I mean anyone not from their county. The fact that you will always speak English with an accent would count heavily against you anywhere but London or one of the other port cities.

"I have many contacts and can help you get started. It would be up to you, naturally, to build your own reputation, but I would suggest you let people know of your education at Salerno whether you want to practice medicine or not. How would you go about it?"

Uberto thought. He had always had a garden with plenty of supplies. There was also the issue of what would be available in this cold, rainy land.

"Having just arrived in London and knowing no one, I throw myself on your mercy. I would need access to an herb garden, of course. If not my own, then someone else's. And somewhere to see clients – a storefront of some kind, and a workroom with a heat source. Then, all my supplies. I brought nothing with me but clothes and one book. I have money to purchase some things, but I do not know if it is enough."

Signore Cavalcanti grew quiet as he thought. Finally, with a glance at Alberto, he looked Uberto in the eye. "This is what I will do for you. First, you will stay in my house and learn the English language as quickly as you can. Alberto will find a tutor for you because his duties are many and do not allow him the time to tutor you personally. While you are learning, we will set you up with a space in my warehouse – there is a small unused area in the back corner where we can add a door and a hearth – then find whatever supplies you feel you will need. As well, we will go next door to the friars and arrange for you to purchase herbs from them. I do not think they will object to such an arrangement, but if they do, there are others with herb gardens we can speak with. I do not believe my own is large enough to provide you with what you would need, but you may certainly speak with Cook about using whatever grows there.

"I may say 'we' but in reality, I mean Alberto. He is not only my steward but my aide here in London. He will know, or can find, virtually anything you need. I, myself, must leave in three days for the continent on another buying trip for His Majesty. Otherwise, I would help you personally. I will write letters of recommendation to a few I know who may be interested in your services, which Alberto will have delivered when you are open for business.

"One year from today, we will meet again to reconcile accounts. Your room and board I will freely give and would naturally assume whatever medicines my household might need would be provided gratis. To preserve appearances, I *do* use an English doctor, but would like you to be a second opinion. Alberto will instruct him to get his medicines from you, but you will look in before actually making anything, yes? The cost of your tutor, rent on the space, and the purchase of your supplies I will leave in Alberto's capable hands.

If you have not earned enough to completely repay me in that year's time, we will arrange the balance as a loan with a reasonable interest rate. Will this suit?"

"Before I answer, may I ask why you would wish to help me – and in such a generous manner?"

Beside him, Alberto coughed. Signore Cavalcanti's face displayed a sad smile. "It is a selfish reason. I trust *medicos* from home more than I trust these English doctors." He waved his hand as he continued," Oh yes, I know. We're not exactly from the same kingdom. But close enough. I believe my daughter died because of an English doctor's incompetence. She was ill, but it was not the sweating sickness that takes London on occasion. The symptoms were not the same, and there were no other reports of it in the city. Nonetheless, the doctor I called said he believed it *was* the sweating sickness, prescribed a draught, and hastily beat a retreat from the house. She took the draught as prescribed and worsened. Another doctor, the one I use now, said it was the wrong prescription, wrote out another one, yet my daughter died before she could take it.

"I know you can use your magic to see what really is wrong with someone and treat them as they *should* be treated. I will not give away your secret, but I want *my* household to have the benefit."

Uberto understood, agreed and so, we began our lives in London. The first thing Signore Cavalcanti did was tell Uberto to change his name. "You will never get along unless you have an English name. They insist upon calling me 'John,' which is their equivalent to Giovanni. Your name is easier. Call yourself Hubert rather than Uberto."

Signore Cavalcanti left us in Alberto's skillful care. While the renovations on the warehouse were taking place, Uberto spent hours with an English tutor learning the language. Then there was all the time spent first with parchment and pen to make up a shopping list of needs and subsequently with Alberto scouring the city for those supplies. The friars were indeed amenable to selling some of their herbs, but many were not grown in England, and importers from the continent had to be found. Then there was the question of guild affiliation. In order to do business in the city, one *had* to be a member of a guild, and it was generally a question not of *what* you knew but *who* you knew. The Grocers' Guild, which regulated the sale of herbs and spices, was no exception. Signore Cavalcanti cajoled three of his friends into sponsoring Uberto who, after presenting his diploma from the school in Salerno to the guild masters, was readily, albeit a bit grudgingly from a few, admitted to membership.

Three months later, Uberto could speak English well enough to be understood by the educated (no small feat), his small shop in the warehouse was ready, and all supplies stocked. It was a glorious occasion when Uberto personally hung the sign "Ferrara, Apothecary" with its mortar-and-pestle logo, from a hook next to the door.

Chapter Fifteen

Throngs did not initially flock to Uberto's door. While Signore Cavalcanti had made his introductions, most people were pleased with their current apothecary and did not think to try the new man. There was also the jealousy of the other apothecaries to contend with. No one outwardly disparaged or sabotaged Uberto, but they looked down their noses at the Neapolitan interloper, especially some of the older men. However, Uberto made certain to speak up at guild meetings and indeed, taught others some better ways of treating certain illnesses. It took almost four months before Uberto was making medicines for people other than Signore Cavalcanti's household. In the meantime, he continued his study of English with the tutor between visits to doctors and nobility, handing out his calling card to all.

You may not know this, but in those times, apothecaries weren't simply medicine-makers. They also visited the sick and diagnosed illness before prescribing then making the remedy. In this, Uberto was unique. He preferred to be only a medicine-maker. This endeared him to the lower classes, who could not afford the higher fees charged by those who not only made medicine but also made house calls. The best grapevine anywhere is through household staff, and it was these people who spread Uberto's name. His first real customer was a charwoman whose son had fallen ill. She timidly entered the shop one cold fall afternoon, told Uberto she had heard about him through one of the Cavalcanti maids who was her sister-in-law, described the cough and sniffles afflicting him, and gratefully accepted the infused-honey cold remedy Uberto sold her for a penny. That was about a day's wages for her and certainly less than she would have paid anywhere else.

105

This was how Uberto's fortune was made. At first, it was people servants in rich households knew, then slowly, the rich households themselves. It was easy to judge what a customer could afford – sumptuary laws dictated what sort of clothing you had to wear based on your station. Uberto charged accordingly. He did not make enough that first year to completely repay Signore Cavalcanti, but within two years, his loan was paid off. He moved from the Cavalcanti house to his own lodgings a ten minute walk away from the shop and within five years, was able to purchase his own building from a retiring apothecary that had a garden at the back and a small apartment on the second floor. Less than a year later, he hired a woman who knew of but cared nothing about magic, to be both housekeeper and cook, and he felt himself set for life.

At the ripe age of sixty but looking only twenty, Uberto took a wife. Mary was the daughter of one of his herb importers and a witch, albeit of Fire. She had a temper that fit her element, which is probably why her father wanted her married and out of his house. Her dowry was a large one. She and Emma, the housekeeper, were constantly at odds, and I was always amazed that Emma stayed on. I was ignored as much as possible – Mary had no use for a pet, much less a familiar, and she resented how close Uberto and I were. However, their marital bliss was short-lived. Even a witch had problems carrying a child to full term in that time, and she and Uberto's son died in childbirth only a year after they were married. Uberto never fully recovered from that loss and remained unmarried for the rest of his life.

But all was not to be smooth sailing. The sweating sickness hit London hard the year after Mary's death, and despite Uberto's knowledge of herbal remedies *and* the magic infused into them, many of his clientele who could not leave the city when things got bad, died. No one knew the cause, just that it arose during the humid summer months and went away after the first frost. This illness, whatever it was (and no one knows what it was even to this day), would strike so fast, people died before a member of the household could summon a doctor, if one could find a doctor to see you, that is. Uberto's magical immunity protected him, but he still stayed in his shop and apartment as much as possible, disdaining going forth in the streets where he would have to dodge bodies piled up until the morgue workers could transport them to mass graves. His housekeeper was widowed just a few short weeks into the epidemic and moved in with us. She caught the illness doing the shopping at some point, but Uberto was able to nurse her back to health.

Food shortages also were a problem. As you know, weather determines a harvest, and there were many lean years. Uberto had the money to buy whatever was needed in his house as well as that of his housekeeper's daughter, but others were not so fortunate. Emma told horrible tales of people who died of starvation standing in line for food the Crown released from its own stores. We saw on our daily walks the beggar population multiply a hundred-fold at times. My size scared many off, but Uberto would put a coin into outstretched hands of those who cared not whether they died of my bite before starvation took them.

Then there were the whims of the monarch. Uberto had felt comfortable moving to England because it, like most of the rest of the known world, practiced the Catholic faith. But King Henry decided he wanted a divorce and to get his way, forcibly converted England to *his* brand of religion – the Catholic faith, more or less, but *he* was the head of the Church, not the Pope. Seemingly overnight, being a Catholic became a beheading offense. It did not worry Uberto – he could just as easily attend a Church of England service as a Catholic one since he had no care for organized religion, but it deeply affected many of his friends - Signore Cavalcanti included. Those who could leave the country, like Uberto's benefactor, did. Those who could not attended the Protestant church as required by law but in secret, held their masses, all the while holding their breath, hoping no one would turn them in.

This continued until Henry's and subsequently, Edward's death, when Mary took the throne and turned the country once again Catholic. For five short years, the Catholics lorded it over the Protestants, then Mary died, Elizabeth took the throne, and although her religious stance was more tolerant than her three predecessors, the practice of Catholicism was once again against the law. Uberto's business suffered somewhat because he took no side in the religious argument. He attended whichever church he was supposed to and sold his remedies to anyone who came, regardless of their faith. But because he refused to publicly proclaim one faith over another, zealots would not deal with him. He even had to find new suppliers for his bottles and some of his herbs.

It took a few years, but things calmed down under Elizabeth's reign. Trade with the continent once again flourished; money, even for commoners, wasn't as hard to come by. Uberto's shop became very prosperous once more as nobles decided his religious stance didn't matter as much as the quality of his medicines. Of course, everyone, down to the beggars in the street, heard of Elizabeth's ongoing problems with Mary, Queen of Scots. On occasion, the general populace wondered whether Mary would succeed Elizabeth and they would have to change their religious affiliation again. Most of the country breathed a sigh of relief when Mary was executed, but many wept. There were also the rumors that witches had caused the winds to turn against the Spanish Armada set to invade England, but they were never proven, nor was anyone brought to trial.

Life was fairly easy for the upper middle class under Elizabeth. Uberto managed to save enough money to purchase a manor house in the country – for his retirement, he said. He rented it to an acquaintance whose lungs were no longer able to stand the dank London air.

Elizabeth finally died, and to our dismay, James of Scotland took her throne. *Everyone* had heard of his hatred of witches. Indeed, many of the learned had read his *Daemonologie* and took its words to heart. While most of the people he had persecuted and prosecuted were female, men did not escape his fear. He brought that fear with him to the English throne, changing Elizabeth's laws from a tolerant stance to one of intolerance. Many of Uberto's customers now came to view his medicines with a jaundiced eye. *How* were they so effective when his competitors' were not? It was time for Uberto to retire to his country home. Slowly, over the course of a couple of years, Uberto caused his appearance to age, affecting a wasting disease that for some reason, his own medicines could not help. His business fell off – who wanted medicines from someone who could not heal himself? But that was the plan all along.

His tenant had passed, probably from tuberculosis, the year before, and Uberto had not re-rented his home. Selling his business at a loss to a man who had apprenticed with a competitor, he settled a sum on Emma's daughter for taking care of her mother, who was still active even in her seventies but did not want to move away from her family, and we made the move to Warwickshire, not far from the childhood home of that man you call the Bard. As soon as we left the city, Uberto shed his disguise and once again, looked like a hale man in his fifties.

The house was, by standards of the time, small. What had attracted Uberto was its seclusion. It was set in a clearing in a forested area and could not be seen either from the road or the neighbors. It was not majestically landscaped, with only a curved driveway in front of the house and a garden between the house and stable. Only a cook and maid were really needed, but the cook had convinced Uberto to hire her son as a coachman and handyman – Uberto had to buy a coach and a second horse. All three knew of Uberto's magic and my role. They had been found by word-of-mouth through the magical community and were magical themselves.

After so many years living in cities, we reveled in the freedom of the countryside. After speaking with Cook about what vegetables and herbs she would like grown, Uberto rolled up his sleeves and set about making the garden his pride and joy. His tenant had neglected it so it took some time to clear, even with the use of magic. It was mid-summer and not a lot could be planted that would be ready for harvest in the fall, but that would change the next year. I enjoyed being a familiar and dog, helping Uberto move earth, and occasionally chasing rabbits and deer. When Cook decided she wanted one of them for dinner, I obligingly – and humanely – killed more than I could eat, although Leonard, Cook's son, had to dress them for her. Lack of opposable thumbs made that impossible for me, and it was not one of Uberto's skills.

Although acting almost the hermit, Uberto still kept up with what was happening around the country and in London, specifically. His correspondence was voluminous, and it took him several hours each morning to read and respond to all his letters. The growing fervor for hunting witches worried both of us. It was no longer confined to the villages, but had spread through cities and countryside alike.

Our idyllic life was rudely interrupted four years after we moved. The local vicar, an old man who loved his parishioners and turned a blind eye to their practices outside the Church, died, and his replacement was a young man with political aspirations, eager to make his name in the diocese and higher by finding witches and bringing them to "justice." As with all such, the accusations started with one old woman, who accused a neighbor, who accused their neighbor, and so on. Finally, an eye was turned toward Katherine, the maid. We never did find out *exactly* what she was accused of, but to save her own skin, she named Uberto. He was a prime target – a man who lived alone, only attending church when required, took no part in any other local activities, *and* had a dog who never seemed to age and was black to boot. Obviously, I was a demon of some sort. One early afternoon, Leonard threw open the door to Uberto's study without waiting to knock or be given permission to enter and delivered the news breathlessly. He had, at his mother's urging, kept an eye on what was happening in the village.

We had already discussed the possibility of this happening, and Uberto had made plans for its eventuality. Everyone knew there was no exoneration in these sorts of proceedings and he had no wish to undergo the questioning, sham trial, and hanging. We agreed that although he probably had many good years ahead of him, he had lived a long life with few regrets. He had purposely made no will so no suspicion would fall on another person. His property would revert to the Crown on his death. Envelopes with cash were left on the kitchen table for Cook and Leonard, hopefully enough to see them through until other employment could be found. He divided what had been in the envelope for Katherine between the other two before sealing them.

The moon was full that night, and as if anticipating some horrible occurrence, the woods were silent. Out in the quiet garden amongst his beloved plants, Uberto cuddled me as if I were a puppy one last time, then drank his potion of mandrake root and poppy juice, enhanced by his magic. He fell asleep before the poison took full hold and did not know of his struggle to breathe, although I was awake for all of it until he took his last breath.

Chapter Sixteen

Although I know I was born and undoubtedly spent time with my mother, my first clear memory of the next life is of the cacophony of a marketplace assaulting my ears. I felt myself being carefully cradled in small but roughened hands. The voice of an older human admonished, "I do not understand why you feel the need for a pet. You do not have enough time to take care of it."

A much younger voice, probably belonging to the hands holding me, whined, "I want *one* something to call my own. I will find the time to take care of him."

"Very well," the older voice replied. I heard the sound of coins clinking together. "The boy wants this one."

"Thank you, master," the younger voice said. "I will take very good care of him. What do I feed him?"

Another, older voice answered. "In the wild, they eat fruit, nuts, and seeds. All of which you would normally have shipboard."

The small hands cradled me to a small chest, and we started moving. I felt myself rumbling, similar to a cat's purring. On closer inspection, I had wings with green feathers. So, a bird of some kind.

To make a long story short, my human was a young boy named Richard, aged about twelve. He had been sold into slavery three years earlier, serving as cabin boy aboard the *Lady Anne*. Richard was one of the lucky ones – although he had a hard life (as is any life aboard a seagoing vessel), the ship's master looked fondly on him, and he was well-treated by the entire crew.

I was a black-billed amazon, or parrot, native to the island of Jamaica. Like many things from the tropics, colorful birds were popular exports to the more northerly countries and freely traded. Richard's master had purchased me from one such trader. My feathers were mostly various shades of green, with a patch of red on one wing, and on the top of my head. I suppose I was chosen as a

111

pet because, as parrots go, I would not grow very large, meaning I would take up less room and eat less than a larger bird. I was named Iguaca, a Taino word meaning "green bird" that Richard had heard in Hispaniola.

Our first two years together were that of a boy and his pet bird. The ship sailed the Caribbean, transporting goods like tobacco and sugar between ports, and trading their own handiwork, such as sails and ropes, with other ships. This was not a pirate ship. The master operated under a license from His Majesty, King James I. That is not to say there were no pirates in the Caribbean at that time. There were plenty, and the *Lady Anne* had her fair share of battles with them.

Richard helped the cook in the galley, ran food to the seamen on duty and to the captain in his cabin, delivered messages from one end of the ship to the other, and any other duties *anyone* could think of for him to do. I spent most of my time perched on his shoulder or somewhere in the rigging. When he slept, curled on a pile of burlap sacks in the corner of the berthing compartment, I roosted on a small chest in his corner.

Richard was accompanying the cook on a shore excursion to purchase foodstuffs when his magic erupted. Almost quite literally. We were on the island of Trinidad, up in the hills where the cook traveled to purchase fresher meat than could be found in the market in the port, when Richard and one of the farm hands got into an argument. Both had just hit puberty and hormones raged as the farm hand teased Richard about his small stature. Before the cook or farmer could intervene, fists flew. I felt the warning signs of magic but could not act fast enough to dampen Richard's anger. The ground trembled.

Everyone stopped, mid-conversation, mid-punch, and looked up the hill to see mud bubbling at the very top of the mountain. Although Richard had *almost* moved from anger to fright, I quickly tamped down on what remained of his anger. The earth shaking stopped, and slowly, the mud subsided back into its crater.

"That was a close one," the farmer told the cook. "If it continues, we may not be here the next time you come."

"What *was* that?" the cook asked.

"That is The Devil's Woodyard," the farmer replied. "It is a mud volcano. It has never completely erupted in my lifetime, but we do have occasional tremors and mudslides. The mud is prized by women in Europe as a beauty product, and my neighbors sell it to traders."

The cook shrugged. Products for women did not interest him. He went back to haggling with the farmer for several goats to be slaughtered and salted.

In the meantime, Richard had completely forgotten his argument with the farm hand and stared, mesmerized, at the top of the mountain. "Never seen a volcano, arsworm?" the farm hand teased.

Ignoring the insult, Richard turned to his tormenter. "Never this close and never one that spit mud."

"But you've seen other volcanoes?" The farmhand forgot the argument, too.

"Yes. There are a few on Hispaniola. But I've only seen them from port, and only a little smoke from the top."

While they were talking about volcanoes, I was frantically trying to get Richard's attention. He needed to know his anger was the cause of the tremor. I pecked his ear, only to be dislodged from his shoulder. I flew back and pecked again. "Stop that! What has gotten into you?" He was not happy with me. I had no choice but to resort to projecting images to him which, I knew, would give him a headache until he accepted my presence in his mind. I started projecting an image of him fighting with the farmhand with a little of the anger he had felt, then an image of the volcano starting to bubble. Adding a little more anger to the feeling, I projected an image of a lava volcano completely erupting.

The cook, having concluded his business with the farmer, grabbed the boy by the arm and started hauling him back down the path to the port. I flew alongside, continuing my projections. Richard started moaning as the headache gained in intensity.

"*Talk to the boy,*" I heard.

"But how?" I replied to the voice, which was that of my mentor, the Head of the Familiars' Council.

"*You know how he thinks to himself. In words. Project words rather than images.*"

I stopped the images and waited for the boy's headache to subside a bit. Then, thinking about how superstitious he was and how he might react to a voice in his head, decided perhaps I should wait until he was alone. There was that, and the fact that I had never "spoken" to one of my charges before. This would be a new experience for me, as well.

"Speaking rather than imaging is a skill that comes with age. You are now old enough and should be able to master it. Contact me when you wish to begin, and I will help you through it."

I waited until that night when Richard was standing watch by himself on the foredeck. The closest sailor was up in the crow's nest and would pay no attention to what was happening below him unless an alarm was raised. Perching on Richard's shoulder, I nuzzled him as I usually did after being fed a treat of fresh fruit and, with my mentor coaching me, started.

The parrot rumbled, a sign of contentment. "Hello, my human," I began.

Richard started, staring around himself and opening his mouth as if to cry out.

"No, no, do not cry out. You are not crazy, nor hearing demons of the deep. You are a wizard, and I am your familiar." I nuzzled him again.

Shock permeated his brain. He completely forgot his surroundings, his duty, even the parrot digging its claws into his shoulder pad. I sent wave upon wave of calming energy until he came to himself again.

"Who *are* you?" he whispered.

"You think of me as a pet," I replied, hopping off his shoulder and onto the ship railing.

He peered at me in the gloom. "Are you *speaking* to me? *What* are you?"

Even using words, this was going to be harder than I had thought. "A lesson, then. You know of witches and wizards, yes?"

Richard nodded. "Yes. The others have whispered of them. They say there are women who can control the winds, others who will curse a rival for money."

"Not all can control the winds, nor do all curse. Not all are female, or witches. Some, like you, are male and are called wizards. Just like regular people, there are good magic users and bad magic users. Some lucky witches and wizards get a familiar, like you and me."

His eyes lit up. "You mean I can make magic? *I* could control the winds?"

"Unfortunately, no. Only Air elements can control the winds. You are Earth. As am I. I will explain, if you can listen to me while keeping watch. And you may *think* rather than speak to me. I will hear your thoughts. It would not do to have someone thinking you are talking to yourself."

Richard shook his head, but to give him credit, the next statement was thought to me, rather than spoken. "This is strange but until I am proven crazy, I will listen. It will at least make the watch go faster."

For the rest of his four-hour watch, I gave him a lesson on magic, what happened and *could* happen when he lost his temper, and the role of familiars. By the time he was relieved and went below to his bed, his head was swimming with new and unfamiliar information.

"Sleep," I told him, and sent more waves of calming energy until his mind quieted enough for him to drift off.

While he slept, I pondered our situation. First, he was an Earth wizard surrounded by water and air. Second, there was no one aboard to teach him. All my previous humans had had mentors.

"*You know the Universe arranges things to suit itself. Perhaps you are meant to teach the boy, yourself. Perhaps circumstances will arrange for a human teacher. Time will tell.*"

My mentor was wise, having thousands more years' experience than me, and I was one of the older familiar spirits. I would teach Richard as best I could and trust the Universe.

The following morning, as he was helping to repair sails, I perched on the deck railing and began his lessons. "Notice the material you are working with," I told him.

"Yes. Linen. What of it?"

"It is a natural fiber, from the flax plant. Remember I told you we are of the Earth element? That means we work with things *from* the Earth.

"Feel the material between your fingers. Look at the way the threads are woven together. Smell the fresh pieces you are using as patches. In other words, get to *know* the material. Once you think you have a good grasp of what the material is, rather than simply sewing the patch on, imagine the fibers of the patch and the sail twining and bonding together."

I could feel the doubt in his mind, but nonetheless, Richard screwed up his face in concentration. While keeping an eye out to ensure no one would see him *not* sewing, I watched in the background as he followed my instructions. Slowly, he understood what I was telling him, and in a short time, I could see him attempting to bond the fibers of the two pieces together. He was unsuccessful, but I did not expect much on the first try.

"You almost had it. Now, so you do not get into any trouble, I suggest you perform the repair everyone expects you to make. We will practice again tomorrow," I told him.

So, our days were spent doing his mundane chores, slipping in lessons where I could. He finally mastered bonding the fibers of both linen sail and hemp rope, covering up the magic with stitching and obvious splicing. Quietly and over time so it would not be quite so apparent, he learned to straighten the wooden door to the berthing compartment, which had been warped so badly by humidity that it would no longer close.

His skills were noticed by the Boatswain who, in turn, recommended to the Captain that Richard be promoted from cabin boy to seaman and be tasked with sail and rigging repair. The Captain agreed, saying Richard could assume those duties as soon as another cabin boy could be found, which happened the next time we made port in the form of a young runaway who had a romantic ideal of life at sea.

Richard, being a slave, could be disposed of at will and, about two years into his life as a full seaman, was sold to a sailmaker in Princes Town, Trinidad. (I understand he commanded a high price – word of his skills had spread throughout the Caribbean.) The sailmaker only accepted me after Richard pointed out that I could fly up into the mountains to get my own food.

Our life changed, and not necessarily for the better. Master Johnathan, observing Richard at work the first day, discerned the magical bonding of the fibers beneath the stitches. "Yer a wizard!" he exclaimed. Richard had no choice but to answer in the affirmative, and we held our collective breath. It could mean death, especially for a slave no one would miss. Instead, the Master rubbed his hands together in glee. "My repairs will be the best in all the Caribbean. Word will spread, and I'll be rich!"

Richard was tasked with *all* sail repairs. Word did spread, and Master Johnathan's coffers filled quickly, due to the quality of "his" patches.

But Richard's health suffered. He worked from sunup to past sundown seven days a week, working by candlelight after dark. Even drawing from the energy around him and with me boosting his magical ability as much as I could, his eyesight started failing, and his ability to direct energy faltered.

"I must get out of here before he literally kills me," Richard said to me late one night as he lay on his pallet. "But how? He keeps me under his thumb day and night."

I privately agreed. The way Richard was deteriorating, it would not be long before he died, and I would find myself in yet another body, as familiar to another witch or wizard. I was not yet ready to make that transition.

"There is a way, but it may end up with your death rather than freedom," I said.

"I will die anyways if I do nothing. Tell me your idea."

"The Boatswain for the *Galicia* seems to be an honorable man, unlike others who have come into the shop. If you can speak with him quietly, you may be able to trade your services for passage aboard their ship."

What I did not tell him is that the bosun was a wizard. His aura said as much. I was counting on the camaraderie often found between magical creatures in an unfriendly environment. It helped that said bosun had a familiar, a seagull, to whom I could speak.

"Passage aboard their ship to where? Then what would I do?"

"Ships always have ports of call, and those ports always have people and places of supply. Change your name and try to obtain employment with whatever chandlery is in wherever the *Galicia* drops you."

He chewed on this for a while. "I believe it is worth the risk. The worst Master Johnathan can do is kill me, but that would be faster than his current method. I will somehow manage to speak with the bosun the next time he comes in."

Within the month, the bosun had come with a couple of sails to be repaired and an order for a new topsail. While Master Johnathan went into the storeroom to check his supplies, Richard drew the bosun aside, presumably to discuss the repairs but in reality, to ask for help. I spoke to the seagull, explaining our predicament and asked his assistance, which he readily gave.

"'Twill be difficult, laddie," the bosun whispered to Richard. "The captain doesna care for the likes o' us."

Richard's eyes widened. "The likes of us?"

The bosun's eyes twinkled. "Aye. Your familiar has spoken with mine, so I ken what ye are, despite yer tryin' ta hide it. An' I can see yer in a bad way here, just by the way your looks have changed since the last I saw ye.

"Be dockside at eight bells of the last dog watch. I'm not the only wizard aboard the *Galicia*. We'll smuggle ye aboard. Ye can stay in our berth 'til we reach Port Royal, and we'll smuggle ye off the same way. Yer on yer own after that, though. I dare not jeopardize me position."

Richard nodded and whispered, "*Thank you*. I will see you this evening, then," and changed the subject to the repairs to be made to the sails just as Master Johnathan re-entered the shop with a sail in his arms.

That evening, as soon as Master Johnathan's snores echoed from his room above the shop, I followed Richard out the window and down to the docks, arriving a few minutes past the appointed time, which was 10:00 p.m. for you, a landlubber.

The bosun and his friend threw a rope ladder over the railing of the *Galicia*. Richard, being no stranger to ships, quickly climbed up. "This way, laddie," the bosun whispered. I flew up into the rigging and settled with the seagull, following Richard's progress down into one of the berthing compartments through his mind.

Chapter Seventeen

Four days later, Richard had the proverbial cabin fever, having been unable to leave the compartment, despite the open porthole allowing him fresh air and making it easy for me to visit. The bosun and his friend had smuggled food to him, as well as some food for me since I didn't eat the same as the seagull. But it was only four days and that evening, Richard departed the ship at the same time and in the same manner as he had arrived, hiding among the crates and barrels on the wharf until daylight.

When the sun was just barely a gleam in the sky, Angus departed the ship, bound for the sailmaker in port. "Follow me," he said quietly as he passed where Richard was hiding. Richard followed behind, attempting to look like a slave following his master. The seagull and I flew above, keeping an eye on the two.

The sailmaker was an old friend of Angus', a countryman named Collum. Collum was a former pirate who had lost his arm to a cannonball shot and retired from the sailing life, using his savings from plunder to set up his own shop. He, like Angus and Richard, was a wizard, so the lack of an arm did not bother him as it might other men of his position. Most pirates are men escaping from *something*, whether it be slavery or a boring life. In Port Royal, it was every man for himself, so Collum did not ask about Richard's status. Once he saw the quality of Richard's repairs, he hired him on as a free man.

Between the two of them, the sailmaking and repair business flourished. Richard grew into his manhood and magic and soon, his skills outpaced those of Collum. Rather than be jealous of Richard's skills, Collum left the manual labor to Richard and focused on the "front counter" work. Unfortunately for Richard, the front counter closed at sunset even though the work was not finished. Collum took himself to the taverns and brothels while Richard worked well past sunset, trying to keep up with the orders. It was not long before Collum left the shop for his leisure activities even before sunset. Richard did not know it because Collum did not share financial information with him, but as fast as Richard increased the profits, Collum spent them.

Five years into their relationship, Richard asked Collum for a raise. After all, he argued, he was doing the majority of the work – not just manufacturing and repairs, but dealing with the customers, too. It seemed only fair that he should have a larger portion of the profits. Unfortunately, he chose an evening after Collum had returned from the taverns to make his request.

"Ye cheeky lad," Collum growled. "Ye'd be nothing without me. I gave you your start."

"And I am grateful for it," Richard soothed. "But as I said, if I am doing the majority of the work, is it not fair that I should make more money?"

Collum's face got redder, if that was possible. Although I could not tell because he was not my wizard, I was afraid of the consequences of his temper. I conveyed as much to Richard, who privately agreed with me. "But I am determined to be treated fairly," he told me.

"If ye think yer worth so much more money, ye can take yerself elsewhere to try and get it," Collum shouted. "Get out of my shop and my life!"

This came as a blow to Richard. He had not thought Collum would be so unreasonable. Knowing asking for the money he was already due would have been futile, he packed up his belongings into a bundle and left the shop, listening to Collum's raging the entire time. We made our way to the wharf, which was the only place Richard could think of to go. I tried to soothe Richard's feelings as best I could, but this was one of life's lessons.

"What will you do now?" I asked.

"Trying to find another job with one of the other chandlers will be fruitless," he replied. "Collum will say bad things about me to everyone he knows. While I *think* my reputation will survive, I do not wish to deal with his rumor-mongering, or his temper. Port Royal is small, and we undoubtedly would run into each other. I know you prefer land, but I think it best if I get away for a while. Like on a ship. I'm good at what I do. I should be able to get a berth with someone."

Richard spent the rest of the night curled up behind some crates, giving me permission to fly up into the mountains to eat my native food. It might be a while before I had that chance again, so as soon as I felt him doze off, I took it. Not wanting to be parted from him for too long (and wanting my own sleep), I flew to a spot I knew well, ate my fill, and returned quickly. I settled myself on top of his bundle and slept until I felt him stir just as dawn was breaking.

With me perched on his shoulder, we wandered the wharf, reading the names on the ships docked there to see if anyone Richard knew was in port. He thought to check that before just blindly approaching every ship he saw. We were in luck… the *Galicia*, the ship that had first brought us to Port Royal, was in port.

"Ahoy the *Galicia*," Richard called from the dock. "Is Angus still the bosun?"

The men in the rigging paused in their work. A weathered face peered over the railing, working a plug of tobacco around in his mouth. "Nay. He was killed in a skirmish a few years back. Who wants to know?"

"My name is Andrew (the name he had taken when first arriving in Port Royal) and I'm a sailmaker. I knew Angus and was hoping he'd be able to help me get a berth aboard your ship. Would you know if the captain is hiring?"

The man scrutinized Richard, then spat tobacco juice over the side. "Hold a moment. I'll ask for ye."

"I will remind you Angus said this captain, if it is the same one, does not like wizards," I admonished my human.

"I remember. But it's easier to get a job using connections than not. I can hide what I am for a while, if needed."

A voice hollered something about getting back to duties, then a different, weathered face appeared over the railing. This one, although not looking much different than the first, had an air of authority to it. He looked Richard over from head to toe, then spared a glance for me. "If yer wantin' work, I can always use an able-bodied seaman. Come aboard, and we'll talk."

I flew up into the rigging, careful to avoid the work being done, while Richard climbed aboard and stood in front of the man I assumed was the captain. After another look-over, the captain asked, "And why would ye want a job on my ship?"

Richard pulled himself up to his full height, which brought him to the captain's shoulders. "I was raised aboard a ship, learned sailmaking and rope repair. I've been working here in Port Royal with Collum for the last five years, but we had a falling out. Rather than get into constant arguments with him, I thought it best to leave. I knew Angus and through him, your ship. It was worth asking."

"Hold a moment," the captain said and turned to a sailor swabbing the deck. "Find Davey and tell him to come here." The sailor scurried off, and shortly, another man came from belowdeck, and to the captain's side. He smiled when he saw Richard, who smiled back at the familiar face which had accompanied Angus to the chandler shop many times. He did not know Davey was still with the *Galicia* or he would have asked for him after hearing of Angus' demise.

"Davey, this small one here is looking for a job and says he's worked with Collum. Do ye know him?" the captain asked.

"Aye. He's good. I'm not sure how Marty will feel about hands better than his, but I think we should find a place for him."

And so it was that Richard was hired on as a seaman. The repairs to sail and rope (and the covering up of magical repairs) were like second nature at this point, but after almost fifteen years on land, he had to regain his sea legs and remember how to climb ropes. New for him was learning how to be a pirate: the use of muskets, swords, and fists. The *Galicia* traveled the Caribbean, attacking and plundering any ship flying a royal flag, regardless of which flag it flew. While he had been exposed to fighting aboard the *Lady Anne* when she was attacked, as a cabin boy and a small one at that, he took no part in battles. In his training, he failed miserably. All the other men were larger and stronger, and try as he might, Richard was easily overpowered each and every time. During the first such attack aboard the *Galicia*, he watched the fighting from the rigging, staying out of the way of men who were capable of holding their own. After it was all over, he lost his lunch right in front of the captain.

"I see ye've no stomach for fighting," the captain laughed. "Clean up yer mess, then report to me in my cabin."

Richard dutifully cleaned up his sick and sheepishly made his way to the captain's cabin. "How old are ye, lad?" the captain asked.

From my perch in the rigging, I reminded Richard that he would not age as quickly as normal humans. He was somewhere in his mid-thirties at this point, but due to his wizard nature *and* his small stature, looked considerably younger. I received a mental nod in reply.

"I'm not sure, sir," Richard responded. "I think I'm in my twenties."

The captain's eyes widened. "Ye *are* small! I'da thought ye were in yer teens. Well. I have no desire to lose a good seaman, especially one who can keep my sails and rigging in such good shape. From now on, when we attack, ye will keep to the galley with the cook and cabin boy. I'll not reduce your share of plunder so long as ye work just as hard as ye have keeping my ship in shape. But mind, if the bosun says one wrong word, it's off my ship you'll go. I can't afford someone who can't fight *or* work!"

Richard nodded and heaved a sigh of relief. "Aye, captain. And have no worries. I'll keep my part up."

Despite teasing from the other men, Richard more than made up for his lack of fighting skills with his other abilities, and even took on further work by helping the ship's bosun and quartermaster when he could. The organizational skills he had learned out of necessity when working with Collum endeared him to those officers, who took up for him when the other seaman made fun of the "wee boy."

We were a few years aboard the *Galicia*, and when once more in Port Royal, Richard received an offer from the bosun of the *Fanny Mae*, which had lost two of her masts and all sails and rigging in a fight with an English privateer. The captain, a Water wizard, had heard of Richard's prowess and wanted someone who could work with the chandler to hurry the work along. Richard accepted the position, bade the crew of the *Galicia* farewell, and for two months we were, blissfully, on dry land. Collum was still around Port Royal and Richard, forewarned, stayed out of sight on the ship, making his trips to the chandler in the early morning when it was known Collum was sleeping off his nightly escapades.

Those two months flew by quickly (at least for me) and we were once again on the open sea, vying for plunder with other pirates. This time, however, Richard had made known his lack of fighting skills (hiding the fact that he did not like it, anyway) and there was no teasing from his shipmates, especially when his small size allowed him to climb rigging like a monkey, beating every other man to the top when they raced. Again, when not involved with repairs, he helped the bosun and the quartermaster, earning himself the occasional bonus from those men when loot was plentiful.

123

We both relished the rare shore leave, especially if it happened to be in Port Royal, just a few hours' walk from the cool of the mountains. He had not had free time to explore while working with either Master Johnathan or Collum, and we took advantage of the leave to go a few miles inland, away from the bustle of the port and all the water. Prudently, Richard found a recognizable tree on one of his walks and buried his share of the sale of loot underneath it at every opportunity. The few times he caught shipmates going through his belongings for something to steal, he privately laughed at their lack of success, then several hours later so as to avoid suspicion, "rearranged" their linen or cotton clothing in such a fashion they were quite uncomfortable. As a sailmaker, he also knew how to repair clothing. The same sailors who thought to rob him found themselves paying to have their britches altered.

After five years, Richard was offered a position as chief of sail repair on the *Steady*, with a better share of plunder. Five years after that, he transferred again. We changed ships several times in a twenty-year span to hide the fact that he did not age as his compatriots did. For the most part, Richard hid his abilities. While he usually sailed on English ships, the Spanish Inquisition had made its way to the Caribbean, and it only took one snitch to condemn a man. There were, however, a few captains who wielded magic as well as he did, although they were usually aligned with Water. Those postings were the easiest because he did not have to disguise anything he did from their eyes.

Richard's last shipboard post was aboard the flagship of a fleet commanded by Sir Henry Morgan, who had a letter of marque from the English governor of Jamaica to attack and plunder any Spanish ships it encountered. This time, rather than being a simple sailor, Richard was the bosun, responsible for all activities on the ship.

Sir Henry, while technically English, was actually a Welshman. The Welsh are fond of the paranormal in any regard, and Sir Henry was delighted to find that his bosun was a wizard – then disappointed when he was told Richard aligned with Earth, not Air or Water. Nonetheless, he made use of Richard's abilities, not only in sail and rigging repair, but helping the ship's carpenter. I was put to work as a scout, being able to rapidly convey information regarding enemy positions to my wizard, and thence to the admiral.

For three years, we sailed between Central and South America and throughout the islands, attacking not only Spanish galleons but

Spanish-held cities, as well. Despite his value to the admiral and his fleet, Richard was expected to take part in any fighting. With a little practice between fighting, his magic finally served him in that capacity. Because metal is an Earth element, he was able to effectively shield himself from musket fire by diverting the bullets, and in close quarters, his opponent would find the edge gone from his sword. Bruises, while still painful, were less fatal than the slash of a cutlass.

Magic, however, could not protect Richard from the consequences of cannon fire when he did not see the danger coming. During the famous attack on La Ceiba, Venezuela, a cannonball struck the mizzenmast, exploding it. I had been perched in that mast's rigging and barely flew off in time. Sadly, there was no time to warn my human. A large chunk of wood pierced his leg. With my help, Richard was able to stem the flow of blood, but the damage was still massive. The ship's surgeon subsequently amputated Richard's left leg just above the knee.

When Morgan and his fleet returned to Port Royal a month later, Richard took his leave of the seafaring life. Collum had literally drunk himself to death and more than twenty years later, few remained who would remember Collum's helper, anyway. With his share of over twenty years of plunder dug up, Richard set up his own shop. His skills were such that word spread quickly, and he soon turned away work.

It took almost a year, but we finally fashioned a *comfortable* prosthetic leg from wood, hemp, and linen. It allowed Richard to escape the bustle of Port Royal, hiking into the mountains. I flew with abandon in my native environment.

It was during one of these hikes that Richard met Yuiza. She was the daughter of the local healer and was out gathering medicinal plants for her mother. The first meeting was brief – Yuiza took one look at Richard and ran away. Richard did not blame her. The Spaniards had enslaved or killed the majority of the native people and despite his skin being as dark as hers, she would not have known he was neither Spanish nor a slave trader.

That did not deter him, though. He thought her beautiful and wanted another chance to get to know her. Delaying some of his work, he timed our next hike to coincide with the same phase of the moon as the first, hoping to see her again.

Luck was with him. When he saw her, he called out to her in the halting Spanish he had learned over the years that he meant no harm. She, naturally, was wary but eventually, they formed first a friendship, then fell in love. Richard's magic was no barrier to their relationship – the Taino and Maroon who lived in the mountains had a deep relationship with the earth and had many shamans amongst them – Yuiza's mother was one.

They married according to Taino custom and Yuiza came to live with us in Port Royal. Over the years, Richard and Yuiza had two boys and a girl, all of whom showed magical ability. Richard and I taught them as best we could, but their education was supplemented by Yuiza's people whenever we visited.

Chapter Eighteen

It was on one of these visits that disaster struck. It was late morning. Richard and I were out in the fields with the men while Yuiza was back in the village, helping to prepare the midday meal. The ground began to tremble, then shake violently. The fields, so carefully terraced over the years, started sliding as a single unit downhill. The men who were in the middle of the fields slid along with the mountainside. Those, like Richard, who had been along the periphery discussing crop yield, stumbled and fell, unable to maintain their balance. As the tremor subsided, I was directed to fly back to the village to check on the women and children.

Most everyone in this village escaped death, but the bodies of some of the men who had been in the fields were never found. The destruction of property and crops was extensive. After a short consultation that night, it was decided Yuiza and the children would stay in the village while Richard and I ventured back into Port Royal. Or what was left of it. There was a spot on our normal path where one could stand and admire the view of the harbor and, farther out, the city of Port Royal. We paused this day to note the area where Richard's shop had been no longer existed. As a matter of fact, the majority of what had been Port Royal was no longer there. What remained was no longer a peninsula, but an island. It took several months, but Richard was able to relocate his business to the new port of Kingston.

They all knew Richard would outlive Yuiza. To stave off suspicion from strangers, they used a spell learned from my mentor to make Richard seem to age. The spell was difficult to maintain, so Richard only used it during the day.

It was the difficulty of maintaining the ageing spell that made them finally decide to sell the sailmaking business and live permanently with Yuiza's people up in the mountains. Their children, now grown, had left the island for more lucrative careers in other parts of the Caribbean, so there was nothing holding them in Kingston.

Once the sale of the business had been concluded to another bosun who had forsaken the sailing life, they made the long trek on foot, hauling their belongings up the mountain. With Richard's help in weaving the cane, a hut was quickly built for them near Yuiza's sister, who had taken over the healer duties from their mother.

They had over fifty years together, but nature finally took Yuiza from Richard. Following custom, she was buried underneath the hut they lived in. While it initially felt odd to someone who had been more-or-less raised on a ship with sea burials, it comforted him to know she was close.

By this time, the town had adopted Richard as one of their own. Like most of the Maroon, Richard was a former slave. He had never been legally freed, but no one who knew him as the cabin boy on the *Lady Anne* would have recognized him – had they even still been alive. As Yuiza's husband, the Taino embraced him. He spent quite a bit of time helping the planters by moving dirt and encouraging the plants. His prosthetic leg had been replaced many times by local wood carvers, each more elaborately decorated than the last.

Life was not all bliss there in the mountains of Jamaica. Apart from hurricanes that threatened life and limb as well as property, there was unrest between the Maroon and the Taino who lived with them, and the British. As they did in other parts of the world, the British pushed their influence as far as they could, taking land from the native population, killing where deals could not be made.

Four short years after Yuiza's death, Richard again found himself embroiled in a war, this time on land, and this time against the British. It was a totally different environment for him. The mountain terrain made direct assaults nearly impossible, so it was a series of sniper attacks and skirmishes. I once again provided aerial reconnaissance, relating what I saw to Richard, who told the commander of the Maroon forces.

It was during this period that the British established the first coffee plantation only a scant four miles from the town where we lived. Seeing the potential in this new crop, several plants were…relocated… by one of Richard's neighbors after a treaty was signed between the warring parties. Together they nurtured the plants and within four years, were able to start selling their beans in Kingston.

Richard's business partner passed his share onto his son, and he onto his son. Together they grew their plantation into one of the largest on the island. Preferring to stay in the background, Richard allowed his partner to conduct all the business while he tended to the agricultural side of things. He was at peace among the plants, and I was able to indulge the wild side of the parrot.

Hurricanes were a fact of life in the islands. Mature coffee plants can withstand nearly everything but a direct hit. Despite my admonishments that Air was *not* his element, Richard attempted to create a dome of air over some seedlings to protect them during fierce winds during one of these storms, when an uprooted tree smashed into his skull, killing him instantly.

I returned once again to the ether to await my next assignment.

Chapter Nineteen

The air was hot and dry when I next awoke back on this plane. I was once again a dog, nursing with my siblings in a nest my mother had made underneath a stand of prickly shrubs. There was a lot of human noise in the area and as I peered around, I could see a circle of tents with three women tending cooking fires; three children amused themselves with sticks and rocks near one of the tents. The smell of roasting meat permeated the air. I fell asleep and was next woken by louder conversation, this time including male voices. Men covered in dirt were coming down from the hills, pickaxes and shovels over their shoulders.

When I was finally weaned from my mother, it was time to learn about my life as it currently was. I was in a mining camp. The men, six of them and all brothers, had a claim on this part of the mountains. They had first found gold, then silver and were quickly on their way to getting rich, assuming no one else found out about their spot and claim-jumped. Unusually, three of them had brought their wives and children with them to the camp. Families were generally left at home, but these women did not mind the hardships of camp life and living as they did rather than back in a town certainly saved money. There would be time to enjoy the finer things in life when the claim paid out. At least, that was the plan.

The humans and dogs did not have it easy. In addition to water having to be hauled up from the valley, venomous snakes were everywhere. I lost four of my five siblings to rattlesnakes when they wandered away from the camp and paid no attention to what was on the ground near them. The men took turns each week going farther up the mountain to shoot a bighorn sheep for food. When seen and killed, the snakes were also roasted, adding a little variety to the menu.

The children were, as you might imagine, rather wild. One of the wives taught "school," teaching them to read from a well-worn Bible and to write with sticks in the dirt. But she had other duties as well and the schooling only took up a couple of hours each day. The rest of the time, they were free to play. The girl, a red-headed child with a temper to match, was the oldest and ring-leader. She could most often be found leading the boys on snake hunts or climbing the pinyon juniper trees to "keep an eye out for claim-jumpers." *This* was my human, and I started following her, attempting to join in the play. She just laughed, scratched my ears when I was near, and teased me when I barked at her from the base of a tree she was perched in.

Rebecca finally accepted my friendship, and we became inseparable. I even slept curled next to her at night, over her mother's objections. Normally, camp dogs had to scavenge their own food and water, but Rebecca ensured I got table scraps and there was a pan of water for me inside the family tent where my mother and remaining sibling were not allowed to go. She named me "Cruz," a short form of the Spanish word *cruzado*, which means mongrel. It fit. No one knew what breed any of the dogs were.

Rebecca's father was the next-oldest of the six brothers and in charge of the family finances. It was his job to make a trip into town about once a month, traveling in a roundabout manner so no one knew where he came from, to cash in their findings and deposit the money into a bank account. One evening, the brothers were sitting around the fire, sorting the hunks of metal to determine what should be taken to the assayer's office. The children were also in the circle, eyes wide as chunks of metal glittered in the firelight. Although they knew they should not touch, one lump of silver caught Rebecca's eye, would not let go, and she reached for it. One of her uncles slapped her hand away, and without warning, that same nugget flew into the uncle's forehead, giving him a bruise. Rebecca calmly picked it up, turning it this way and that to admire the shininess. Everyone turned to look at Rebecca in stunned silence. Everyone, that is, except the oldest brother.

He sighed. "John, it appears your daughter has inherited Dad's affinity for metal." The other five brothers turned to him with inquisitive looks on their faces. He noticed, then sighed again. "Yeah, I know you don't know anything about it. Mom and Dad made me promise not to say anything to anyone because none of us had his magic."

With the word "magic," gasps came from the entire camp. Rebecca's father said, "I think you had better explain." Even the women found a place around the fire, and all sat to listen.

"You know Dad worked as an ironworker for the Central Pacific Railroad in their locomotive shop, right?" They all nodded. "One of the reasons he was so good at it and kept getting promoted was his ability to detect flaws in the iron so nothing that could become dangerous left the shop. With effort, he could even fix some of the flaws. His magic wasn't strong, and since he had to keep it hidden, he didn't use it much. But he had it, all the same."

"How'd you find out about it if none of the rest of us knew?" John asked.

"I caught him fixing a crack in one of Mom's frying pans when I was about fifteen. Since I was past puberty and so were you, John, Dad reckoned we hadn't inherited it. He made me promise to keep my mouth shut unless I saw one of the rest of you do something. It must've skipped generations."

"*Magic,*" Rebecca thought. "*I have magic. How wonderful!*" While the adults were conversing, mostly about her, she tuned them out, and her imagination took hold. She thought about flying like the proverbial witch on a broom, about turning herself into any sort of animal she wished, and other flights of fancy. I had to stop her from thinking in those directions – they did not correspond with her element. Overriding her musings, I projected images of silver melting into shapes like a flagon or serving platter, a lump of gold fluidly morphing itself into a ring, and the sides of a crack in an iron frying pan flowing back together to form a seamless whole once again.

Of course, my intrusion into her brain caused a headache. And of course, no one knew why she had a headache. When she complained, her mother made her a tisane and sent her to bed. I crawled in next to her and sent calming energy until she fell asleep. I would try again the next day.

There was no time to get her used to me the next morning. The adults had stayed up talking until the wee hours of the morning, deciding what to do about Rebecca. It was the day her father was to leave on his trip to the assayer's office, but this time, the trip would be longer. Once he had sold the gold and silver for the brothers' account, he would purchase a horse and buggy and take her to Los Angeles, where they would catch a train for Sacramento and the

132

grandparents. Rebecca would stay and learn about her magic from her grandfather, and her father would return to the mine. It took a lot of wheedling on Rebecca's part, but I was finally allowed to travel with her.

Her father did indeed take a long route into town. Instead of heading directly southwest, we walked north from the site, through two passes in the mountains, then approached the town from the northwest. It was an all-day trip and despite the resilience of the young, Rebecca was tired and whiny by the time they strode into San Bernardino at dusk. They stayed in a hotel overnight, went to the assayer's office first thing in the morning, then to the livery, where her father purchased an old nag and well-used buggy. At least I got to ride this time. It was late afternoon when we pulled up in front of another hotel, this time almost directly across from the train station. In both hotels, I was not welcome, but it was not difficult to find an out-of-the way place to curl up and sleep for one night.

Rebecca's father grumbled when told if they insisted on traveling with a dog, they would have to ride in the freight car. *Genteel folk*, he was told, would not welcome a flea-bitten mutt in their midst. Rebecca started to argue I was *not* such a creature (and I was not) but was shushed by her father. It was only a half day, and they would survive. It was the price she would have to pay if she wanted to take her pet with her, he said. But once underway, her complaints were forgotten. One of the car doors was left open, and she was able to sit near (her father would not let her dangle her feet outside the car) and observe the landscape flying past. She did not remember the trip from Sacramento to the mine several years previous and was enjoying the trip. I would have tried again to get her to accept me in her mind, but she was having too much fun. There would be a better time to do so later.

Nearing midnight, the two walked up the steps of a small house about a mile from the station and at the outskirts of town. Everything was dark – the inhabitants had naturally retired for the night. John knocked loudly, then called. He did not want to be greeted by the business end of a shotgun. After a few moments, a bleary-eyed, white-haired old man with the gaunt face of a sick person in a nightshirt opened the door with a candle in his hand and exclaimed when he saw the father and daughter duo. "John! What brings you...and Rebecca? Here at such an hour? Where is Madeleine?"

133

He motioned for them to enter the house, and once everyone was inside, shut and re-locked the door.

"Sorry, Dad," John said. "It's a long story. Go back to bed, and I'll tell you and Mom all about it in the morning. Can I put Rebecca in the spare room?"

"Of course, of course. You both can stay in there. Your mother purchased a trundle bed last year. There's room for both of you. The dog?"

Rebecca smiled shyly. She barely remembered the man looking down at her. "This is Cruz. He's mine. He sleeps with me."

"Is that so?" the grandfather asked. "Your grandmother might have something to say about that. Perhaps it would be best if he slept on the floor next to you."

At the mention of a grandmother, a woman about the same age as the man but with considerably less gray in her auburn hair, came out of the hall. "What's going on? John? Rebecca? What are you doing here?"

"He says it's a long story, Martha, and will tell it in the morning. I agree. It's late, and they've had a long journey. Go back to bed. I'll light their way to the spare room then join you."

We were ushered into a small room; the grandfather lit the candle on the bedside table then said his good nights. John pulled the trundle out from under the bed, threw a pillow and blanket from the top bed on it, then pulled his boots off and lay down on the bed. "Dad was right," he told Rebecca. "Cruz needs to sleep on the floor until he can have a proper bath, so keep him there." Rebecca crawled onto the bed, and because I could understand what was being said, I lay on the floor next to her. Her hand drifted onto my back, and within minutes, both humans were asleep. I followed shortly thereafter.

The next morning, John relayed the previous three days to his astonished parents. "I don't know what else to do other than have you teach her, Dad," he said at the end. "I'm afraid of just letting her loose with no control. James is sporting a nice bruise, and that was a minor incident. She hasn't outgrown her temper one bit in the four years since we left."

The grandfather sighed. "I am honestly glad magic did not die out in our family. I was worried when none of you boys had exhibited any power. Yes, I will teach her what I know. But John, there isn't much time. We haven't told you in any letters, but I am dying. I caught a lung disease working in the factory that for some reason my body is unable to heal. Usually, witches and wizards are long-lived, but I will not be one of them. The doctors tell me the pain will become worse and my breath will become shorter until one day I will cease to breathe."

John gasped. "Why didn't you tell us?"

"Because there is nothing you can do. I have made my peace and will go to God knowing I've done what I can with the life I've been given."

Martha put her hand on John's. "It's okay, son. I will miss Abraham when he is gone but I, too, have accepted his – and my fate. We thought he would outlive me, but now we know that is not the case. We have six wonderful sons and three lovely grandchildren. Perhaps more in time. You all are working hard to make better lives for yourselves, and I relish that thought. At some time in the future, you will leave the mine and come back to civilization, and I hope at least one of you will live here in Sacramento. In the meantime, I will have Rebecca to keep me company."

John spent the rest of the morning with his parents, knowing it would probably be his last. Rebecca caught the somber mood and was unusually quiet. She and I played out in the yard – I fetched sticks for her. While not the best time, I knew I had to make her understand what I was to her. It did not appear her grandfather knew of familiars, or he would have said something. I once again sent the images of changing lumps of metal into recognizable items, then alternated images of her and me. It took almost an hour and her head was pounding but *finally* she looked at me and said, "You're part of my magic?"

"*Yes,*" I said into her mind and her eyes widened as she heard the word. With an inaudible *snap* our bond was complete and miraculously, her headache disappeared.

She peppered me with questions. "*Calmly, my human,*" I told her. "*First, you may think to me, rather than speaking out loud. It saves explanations to those who do not know of magic – and may save you from a trip to the asylum. Not everyone carries on conversations with their pets, you know.*

"*Secondly, we have a lot of time for you to learn about me and my role. As you heard your grandfather say, witches and wizards normally live long lives. May I suggest you be a good daughter and spend the rest of the afternoon with your father? He will be leaving soon, and you may not see him for a few years.*"

She nodded and went back into the house. Her grandmother was preparing lunch while the two men sat by the fire talking in low tones. She sat on the floor at her father's feet and listened quietly. They were speaking mostly of Martha and Rebecca, and what would happen after Abraham passed beyond. She did not understand most of it, but I knew her presence was comforting to her father.

After lunch was over, John took his leave to catch the train back to Los Angeles. There were tears in his eyes as he hugged his father goodbye. "Perhaps I will make it until your next visit," Abraham told him. "But if not, your mother will care for Rebecca just as she did you and your brothers. Do not fear. I do not."

John had no tears in his eyes when he kissed Rebecca goodbye. "Pay attention to your grandfather in all things magical, and to your grandmother as she teaches you to become a respectable young woman. You have been allowed a great deal of freedom at the camp, but city living is different. Be a good girl!"

Then, he was gone. Abraham took several breaths then looked at Rebecca. "So, my little witch. What would you like to learn first?"

Rebecca became excited and almost danced in place. "Cruz showed me pictures of lumps of gold changing into rings. Teach me to do that!"

Abraham laughed, then coughed hard, steadying himself with a hand on the wall until he could breathe properly again. "Ah. You have a familiar. I have heard of them, although I know of none myself. What you describe is advanced magic. You must learn to crawl before you can walk, then run! How about I tell you the basics, first?"

Rebecca frowned but with a silent admonishment from me, acquiesced. "Okay," she said, rather petulantly.

Over the next three months, Rebecca learned about magic from her grandfather. She was a quick study, and by the end of those three months, was able to mend metal just as easily as her grandfather – with my help, of course. Abraham was about to purchase small lumps of raw copper, which was less expensive than gold or silver, for her to practice on when the pain in his lungs became too great and he took to bed. It was only three days after that he passed on.

Martha, with a teenage girl to raise, did not have time to mourn the passing of her husband. While Abraham had been alive, Rebecca had been allowed to wear the shirts and pants she was accustomed to, although Martha made her wear a blouse and skirt to church on Sundays. Now, however, it was time for Rebecca to go to school, and she *had* to look like a proper girl. She hated it. And hated school. She missed running around the camp with her cousins and found being forced to sit in a chair for six hours each day, listening to the teacher drone, awful. The first day, she tried to run home from school and got her legs tangled in her skirt, landing her in a heap in the road. That was the first time I heard her use the same language her father and uncles had when they thought the children could not hear.

"Damn it all to hell!" she exclaimed. "I hate these skirts!"

Martha got a colorful earful about female dress when Rebecca got home. That earned Rebecca a cuff on the ear. "Ladies do not speak in such a way!" Martha sternly said. "Look. You have torn your skirt. Learning to mend is another skill you need. Change and I will show you how."

Rebecca made a face but did as bidden. While she changed, I quietly told her the skirt was cotton and as a natural substance, could be mended without stitches. I showed her how to draw the threads together, then fuse them. It only took her two attempts, and although not as smooth as her metal repairs, it barely showed. "That's handy," she told me and after she had fixed the tear in her skirt, triumphantly showed it to her grandmother. "I don't need to learn to sew," she hooted.

"You should anyway," Martha shot back. "You need to learn to sew and embroider, which is what ladies do in polite company."

"Later," Rebecca said defiantly. I knew she had no intention of learning such things. "I want to go down to the river for a while." Without waiting for Martha's permission, she ran back to her room, changed into her shirt and pants, and dashed out the door with me at her heels.

She had also lied about where she was going. After Abraham's death, fascinated with the locomotives and all things railroad, she had taken to hanging out at the railroad yard. There were boys, street urchins, who also dallied at the yard. After some reluctance due to Rebecca's gender, which was immediately dispelled when she gave one of them a black eye, they allowed her into their little gang. They did nothing more than lean against a shed or climb into an empty freight car, but it passed time. Rebecca, "Reb" as the boys called her, was teased a little about going to school, but that stopped when she threatened to fight them all. At fourteen, she was taller than all, and feistier than most. She scared them. My baring of teeth probably helped.

So, Rebecca was bored during the day but to her credit, did learn to read, write with a fair hand, and cipher – or do her arithmetic. Martha bargained with her – she could go with her friends three afternoons per week, but the other four, she stayed home and learned to cook, clean, and sew. At least enough that she would not embarrass Martha who, after a year's mourning, started receiving guests and making social rounds.

Chapter Twenty

Then, the unthinkable happened. Rebecca came home from school one day to find Martha sprawled on the kitchen floor, dead. If I had to guess, it was a massive stroke or heart attack. Either way, Rebecca was left without an adult to take charge. The authorities were called, and to Rebecca's horror, she was put into an orphanage until her parents could be located and told. Of course, I was not allowed to go with her and was left to my own devices – they thought. I hung around outside the building, talking to her all the while to keep her calm. It only took one night for her to decide that was where she was *not* going to stay. When the matron had tucked the girls in, turned out the light and retired to her own quarters on the second night, Rebecca put on her shirt and pants, shoved the hated blouse and skirt under her blanket, opened a window, and shinnied down a drain spout to freedom. We ran to the rail yard.

It took about an hour to find where her friends holed up that night. They, along with some hobos, had made a small camp inside a dilapidated boxcar at the far end of the rail yard. Her appearance surprised everyone, but after a brief explanation to Johnny, the leader of their small gang, she was welcomed. The adults were more cautious, looking at her with curious eyes when they thought she was looking the other way. But they would be gone in the morning – either to a job or hopping a train to the next destination in the hopes they would find a job there.

The next morning, Reb (as she decided she would be called) learned about life on the streets. It was up to each member of their gang of five to return to their camp each night with something of value to be shared – food, money, shoes, clothing. This meant she had to learn to be a thief. Johnny took her out into the streets of Sacramento that entire week, teaching her how to find what they needed, and how to take it without being caught. Naturally, rummaging through other people's trash was a priority. Especially in the rich part of town, a *lot* of useful items were discarded on a daily basis.

The first thing Reb needed was a knife. Not only for protection but to cut up food. She found one in an alley next to a trash pile. It had probably been discarded because the blade was nicked in several places. For Reb, however, this was no problem. That night, after everyone had bedded down, she held it under her blanket just in case someone was watching and, feeling along its length, used her magic to smooth the edge and while at it, made it razor-sharp. The next day she cut up an old boot and made a sheath for it. This she tucked into the back of her pants. During the heat of the afternoon when most people were indoors and there was no one to steal from, she practiced throwing it. Within a few weeks, she could hit whatever target she picked. This scared her compatriots even more than her temper.

Over the course of the next few months, Reb ensured she had a steady supply of metal objects to play with. Tin cans were easy enough to come by – all hobos and street urchins ate canned beans and other vegetables on a regular basis. Discarded broken toys were another good source. Small pieces of scrap iron were found in abundance at the rail yard and locomotive factory. These she hoarded at the other end of the rail yard from their camp, and when everyone thought she was down there throwing her knife at various targets, she was actually learning how to work with the different metals. She did, however, throw her knife often enough that a 'thunk' was heard and kept curious eyes away.

About a year after escaping the orphanage, Reb decided she no longer wanted to live on the streets. It was, to be honest, worse than living in the mining camp. At least there, she had regular meals and her mother ensured she bathed at least once a week. Foraging for food meant there was little, and her head itched constantly. She also missed the comfort of living with her grandparents with a roof over her head and a soft bed. It took her several sleepless nights to determine how she would move up in the world.

Sacramento was a booming city in the early part of the twentieth century. Not one but two railroads brought people and commerce. As the capital of California, it was full of politicians, too. There were rich people all over – people with precious metals and stones in the form of jewelry. Reb announced her departure from the gang of five. The boys took it in stride – they would no longer have to share their takings with her, after all. We moved from the rail yard to a copse of trees in a city park. She found at least one discarded newspaper to read each afternoon, soon discovering who was who in the city and where they lived. She started scouting mansions in between trips to the backs of restaurants and grocers to find food for both of us.

Her first foray as a cat burglar was a month after we had moved. She had read of a fancy ball to be held at the Governor's Mansion and knew that the *crème de la crème* of Sacramento society would be there. One of the railroad moguls had a house not far from our park and his staff, at least to her eyes, paid little attention to much of anything when the owners were away. One light only shone in a window at the back of the house. Reb guessed it was the butler, waiting in his office for his master to return. Everything else was dark.

Quietly, she snuck around the back of the house, and after some consternation, figured out how to open the locked door by melting the latch bolt in place, then separating it from the strike plate. There was no 'click' when she opened the door. I was told to stay in the shrubbery at the front of the house and alert her if the owners came home prematurely. I mentally followed her progress through the empty kitchen, up the servants' stairs at the back and into the bedrooms of the master and mistress. It took little time to find their jewelry cases, and she filled her pockets with cufflinks, a watch chain, several of the lady's necklaces, and one pair of earrings. All were heavy gold, and one pair of cufflinks had stones in them, but it was too dark to see what they might be. She had picked everything out by magical feel. Quickly, she made her way back down the stairs and out the door she had come in through.

Her next task was to repair the lock. That, she found, she could not do. Without being able to see, she could not re-form the latch bolt into its original shape. She did the best she could with the bolt, then caused the spring that held it in place to bend. No locksmith would be able to figure out what had happened to it, but she hoped no one would consider magic as the culprit. We hastily made our retreat to the park and, satisfied with her night's work, Reb fell asleep with me curled at her side.

The next morning, after a breakfast of half-moldy bread taken from the back of a bakery three blocks away, she sat with her back to the largest tree in our copse and surveyed her take with a smile. The cufflinks did indeed have red stones in them. Those she pried out with her knife and set them aside to consider later. She would have to go to the library to learn about gems. She turned her attention to the gold. She knew from her father that pure gold was really too soft to make into jewelry – it had to be combined with other, harder metals to hold its shape. It was a painstaking process to melt the metal and separate out the different ones – all without benefit of a forge, but about two hours later she had several lumps that looked very much like what her father and uncles took from the mine and sold to the assayer. These, along with the stones, she buried underneath the tree.

After some conversation, we decided if she was going to live this kind of life, she needed to learn more about locks. We wandered the city until we found an abandoned house on the other side of town. Reb considered it thoughtfully. Not only might it be a good place to practice on locks, it might be a better place to live than the park. That idea, however, was quickly dispelled. When she entered through a broken window, she found evidence that *someone* was already living there. She wanted no argument over who had squatter rights! However, as no one was in sight, she took the locks from two bedrooms, one from the back door, as well as a rusted padlock on a shed in the backyard, and we made our way back to our park.

Over the course of the next two days, she used stolen screwdrivers to take the locks apart and put them back together several times to understand exactly how they worked. Then she did the same thing with magic. The first two times, she managed to fuse the wrong parts together, making the locks completely inoperable. But finally, she managed to open and re-lock each as if she had a key.

During breaks from her practice, in addition to finding food (I was on my own and ate mostly squirrels and birds), she listened behind sheds and fences to household staff gossip and read her scavenged newspapers. There was a report of a break-in at the railroad executive's house, but the police were dumbfounded as to how the burglar managed to break the lock without the butler hearing. That was good news. She planned her next escapade.

Three weeks after the first, she broke into the house of the senator from Los Angeles while he and his wife were back home attending a family funeral. It was quite convenient that the paper reported the comings-and-goings of the rich in the gossip columns! As with the first house, Reb watched the servants beforehand to learn their movements. Again, they were lackadaisical if their employers were away. This time, she had no need to melt anything. She simply moved the tumblers inside the door's lock and slid the latch back, holding it open with magic. Seven minutes later, she was back outside, quietly releasing the latch and moving the tumblers back into their locked position. It was a little noisier than just melting the metal, but the 'click' was barely audible, even to my sharp ears.

The next morning, she repeated her slagging process with the gold. Four more stones of indeterminate type were added to her stash. Her pile was a decent size, and it was time to find an assayer. One, I might add, somewhere other than Sacramento. She knew the one her father and uncles had used, but that was a long way away in San Bernardino. She did not want to travel that far and also did not want to run into them if they were still at the mine. But she knew from hanging around the rail yard that some were still finding gold near the site of Sutter's Mill and assumed there would be at least one assayer in the nearby town of Placerville, to which there was, conveniently, a train. It was time to temporarily relocate.

She put half her metal into a pouch she tucked into her shirt, completely covered her buried stash, picked up her blanket, and we headed for the rail yard. Fearful of running into her old gang and not wanting to answer any questions, we hid out where she had once practiced on tin cans until she heard one of the workers talk about the Placerville run and which track it was on. We moved a little south from our original position, and when said train started to move, jumped into an open boxcar. She spent a pleasant couple of hours chatting with an old hobo who was retiring from the life and moving back "home," until the train pulled into the small station.

Once we disembarked from the train, we had to find an assayer's office. Thankfully, Placerville was much smaller than even San Bernardino, and it only took a short while to find *the* assayer's office. The man looked up in surprise when a young lady walked through his door, but her man's dress along with her disheveled appearance soon had him counting her among the other miners he saw. There was some heated conversation when the assayer wanted to know where she had mined not only gold but silver and nickel. Reb held her ground – and her tongue. Thirty minutes later, she walked out with a little over one hundred dollars in paper and coin in her pocket. She felt rich!

"I am going to get clean, really clean, for the first time in over a year," she told me as we walked next door to the general store. Ten minutes later, she emerged with a new shirt, pair of pants, and a bar of soap. We walked across the dusty street to the saloon, which doubled as a hotel. While I found a shady spot next to the building to lounge in, she got a hot bath and a hot meal – her first in a very long time. Two hours later, she found me and handed me a large chunk of roast beef, which I promptly devoured. It was much tastier than the wild animals and vegetable trash I had been eating.

We were just in time to catch the train back to Sacramento. It was nearly midnight by the time we returned to our copse in the park, and Reb fell asleep almost immediately. I stayed awake a little longer, watching her dream of living in a mansion just like the ones she robbed.

The next morning, she mentally added up her money and the supposed value of what she still had buried. She thought she had enough money to get a room in a boarding house, but I wondered if she might have a problem doing that. First, she was a young lady on her own, which would raise questions. Second, would she have the freedom to come and go at night? I had a point, she conceded, and started to ruminate on where she might live that was independent but at least under a roof.

Her questions were answered within a week. A war had been going on in Europe for a few years, and the president decided to end the neutrality of the United States and enter the war. It was not a popular decision, and in order to raise enough bodies to do this, a law was passed requiring young men to fight. It only took a month for the streets of Sacramento to become nearly empty. All that was left were older men, women, and children. The boarding houses were empty, as well, and Reb had no difficulty talking one woman into renting us a room – one that came with a key to the front door. It also came with breakfast and dinner, and one hot bath a week. I got table scraps every day. Reb's weekly bath was one for me, too, as she pulled me into the tub with her. We both started looking and feeling healthier.

Margery, the landlady, assumed Reb was a call girl (wondering what sort of men would like a woman who dressed like them rather than in skirts), and wondered how she would make her money with all the young men gone off to war. To this, Reb snorted. Not willing to disabuse the notion of her employment, she reminded Margery there were still plenty of men left in Sacramento, and many of those had more money than the ones who had left.

Reb was correct in her assessment of the men, but it was not their bodies she wanted. Anyone who had a lot of jewelry was too old to be conscripted, but many of their male servants were not. That left many a mansion unprotected at night when the owners went to parties, and Reb took full advantage. Within three months, she had more than tripled her stash, which had been moved from the tree in the park to under a loose floorboard in her room.

During those three months, we made two more trips to Placerville. Reb was now indeed a rich woman by standards of the time, although she still looked and acted like an urchin. It suited her to have people look the other way, although her fondness for Margery made her a little sad when she winced every time Reb left the house in men's clothing. No persuasion on her part would make Reb wear skirts.

Although she was good at what she did, Reb did not want to be a thief the rest of her life. She recognized the dangers and knew it was only a matter of time before she got caught. She had to think of another way to make money. She remembered the images I had sent her long ago of gold transforming into the jewelry she now stole and thought perhaps rather than steal it, she could make it. So in her free time, of which there was plenty, she started practicing.

She had kept one ring intact and used this as a model, working with her remaining supply of nuggets. Its small size made it more difficult to mold than the pieces of a lock, not to mention she had to re-combine metals to get a decent hardness, and she was frustrated for quite some time.

Just as Reb thought she had gotten the hang of forming a delicate object, a sickness, now known as the Spanish Flu, hit Sacramento. Hundreds of people succumbed to the disease, and the city became almost a ghost town as residents stayed indoors, attempting to avoid getting sick. I told Reb of her natural immunity to such illnesses, but to avoid suspicion, she had to act as everyone else did and covered her nose and mouth with a mask when she went out.

She was worried about Margery, however. The lady, a childless widow in her fifties, insisted she was going to live her life as usual.

145

She did the marketing on Monday and Thursday and went to church on Sunday. When Reb, citing her youth, offered to do at least the marketing, Margery turned her down flat. Two months after that conversation, despite wearing a mask when outside the house, Margery started coughing and developed a high fever. Before Reb could find a doctor willing to come to the house, Margery's face turned blue, and she suffocated on her own mucus. It was Reb's first exposure to death, and she took it hard, crying as the men from the morgue, wearing masks over their faces, took Margery's body away. One man looked at Reb's tear-streaked face and told her, "We'll be back for you next week." I thought that was rather hard-hearted.

Four days later, a man came to the door. He was dressed in a suit, with the requisite mask over his face, and carried a briefcase. Reb, expecting to be told she had to leave the house, was shocked when she was told Margery had left the house to her. He handed her a letter in Margery's hand. It was dated the day after Reb had volunteered to do the marketing. "Child," it said. "Your offer touched me. No one has cared that much for me since my dear husband passed six years ago. I suspect I will get this Spanish Flu at some point and will probably not survive it. I am not worried. I have had a good life and look forward to meeting God when and if He wills it. I have no living relatives and so, in the hopes that having a permanent roof over your head might persuade you to give up your occupation and become a respectable woman, I am leaving you my house. When the men return, if they have not already, you will be able to rent rooms just as I have. It isn't the best living, but is better than what you are now doing. With affection, Margery Hoffman."

With a stroke of a pen on a legal piece of paper, Reb became a woman of property. The lawyer, a Mr. Moore, looked upon Reb with disdain. He was one of those who did not like women who did not *look* like women, apparently. But he kept to the formalities and asked Reb what would happen to the house if *she* died. Reb shrugged her shoulders. She had no knowledge of the whereabouts of her family; in truth, had no desire to locate them (because she would have to explain herself); and having only owned the house for about ten minutes, cared not what happened to it. When she told him as much, he advised her the State would take it if she did not will it to someone. She shrugged again. Mr. Moore left, disgusted, but told her a deed would arrive in the mail in about two weeks' time, and she should put that somewhere safe.

Chapter Twenty-One

Now without having to pay rent, Reb thought she had enough money to live comfortably for several years, even considering the sum she would have to pay each year that Mr. Moore called a "property tax." In that time, she decided she would perfect her jewelry-making skills and open a shop. I reminded her she would need to practice with a forge. Otherwise, people would wonder how she did it, and although a lot of people knew about magic, it was still kept under wraps.

Together, we thought through the practicalities of each step. The further we progressed, the more it was obvious she could not do as she had imagined. There was nowhere on the property to put a forge, even a small one, nor did she have any idea how to fake using one. Then there was the consideration of a shop. Renting one would cost money, and she did not want to speculate with her savings. After several days of this, she finally hit upon the idea of making her jewelry in the house then traveling to a larger city, such as San Francisco, to sell her wares to people who *did* own shops. After having observed the humans she interacted with over the years, I brought up the subject of her appearance. Men did not like women who did not dress like women, and her gender would make it difficult for shop owners to believe she had forged the jewelry herself. It would, I commented, probably make them assume she was selling stolen goods.

She mused on this, then laughed. "That is easy enough to remedy," she told me. Within a half hour, she had crudely cut her hair into a man's style, using a little cooking grease to slick it down. She cut a sheet into strips, and she bound her breasts before putting her shirt and vest back on. She slowly turned in a circle. "Well?"

I eyed her critically and thought she would pass muster. Although her face was pixie-ish, she had always walked with the long strides of a man, and her voice was relatively deep for a woman. I calculated others would assume she was a man who liked men. "You will need to obtain a hat," I told her. Men always wore hats in those days. "Perhaps a suit, as well. You should look like someone in business, not someone who just arrived from the mining camp."

It took another three months, but Reb eventually made a beautiful ring. Once she figured out how to melt the metals in the proper proportion then form them, it took no time at all for her to build up a stock of rings and brooches. Most had no stones in them, as she had few to begin with. However, signet rings for men and filigree rings and brooches for women were stylish. She acquired a suit and hat, and a case in which to show her wares. On a Monday morning, she boarded a train for San Francisco. I snuck onto a freight car so I could travel with her.

It took her an entire week of trudging through the city, her case in hand, to sell all but four pieces of her jewelry. She did not earn as much as she had thought she would because she had based her estimates on the prices she saw in jewelry stores, not knowing how the supply chain worked and wholesale versus retail pricing. She had also failed to account for her travel expenses – not just the train but hotel and restaurant charges. Her wares were well-received, however, and she did receive several orders for more of the same.

We returned to Sacramento the same way we had come – her in a passenger car and me in a boxcar. Once home, she realized she had another problem – she had used up her remaining supply of nuggets to make this first batch of jewelry. Since she no longer wished to rob houses, she resorted to legitimacy and purchased the raw materials from an assayer. It would not be as profitable as using stolen goods, but she was already fairly wealthy if the pile of paper and coin money under the floorboard in her bedroom was any indication.

Reb continued her jewelry-making business for five years, making the trip into San Francisco three times per year. Although the men returned from war and life as it had been resumed, she rented no rooms as Margery had hoped. Instead, it was just the two of us rattling around the large house. The more she thought about it, the more she no longer wanted something that required so much upkeep. At the end of those five years, she decided to get out of the wholesale business, sell her house, and move somewhere else. The house sold quickly to a couple with a large family. Reb sold the house furnished, packed her few belongings into a suitcase and after nearly ten years, we resumed our lives as vagabonds.

But that life was short-lived, thank goodness. She had already decided where she wanted to live, and it only took a month of living rough before she purchased a small cottage in a town called Emeryville. She had passed through it on every trip to and from San Francisco and with its view of San Francisco Bay, it was a picturesque place. All the structures were relatively new, having been built after the big earthquake a couple of decades earlier, and for the first time in her life, she had indoor plumbing.

Between the sale of the house and her now-defunct jewelry business, Reb no longer *needed* to work but had to have something to fill the hours. She had business cards printed for a custom jewelry business, figuring she would get enough commissions to keep herself busy. These she handed to every jewelry store owner in both San Francisco and Oakland. But before she could make the first piece, the stock market crashed. Jewelry was now being pawned rather than purchased, and after a few months, even pawnbrokers stopped taking it. Reb purchased a few pieces from a broker she knew, saving them for future need, but she held back on acquiring a lot.

She spent the better part of that decade helping where she could in soup kitchens and even purchasing canned goods and passing them out to the people she saw on the street. Her reputation spread, someone figured out where she lived, and soon, she was operating that boarding house Margery had dreamed of – free of charge. Except, her cottage was only two bedrooms. People slept on the floor, and Reb fed whoever came to the door with whatever food she could find. Even food became scarce at times.

Life slowly returned to a semblance of normalcy. The people sleeping on the floor eventually found jobs or moved to other cities for work, and it was once again just the two of us. She renewed her acquaintance with jewelry store owners, although there were far fewer than there had been. She averaged a commission every couple of months, which was enough to keep her hand in but not enough to make it a full-time occupation.

One day when she was working on a piece at the kitchen table, there was a knock at the door. She hadn't been expecting visitors and therefore, had not donned her disguise as a man, leaving her hair natural and her breasts unbound. Without thinking about this, she opened the door to find a man standing there, a bouquet of roses in his hand. It took a few heartbeats, but she finally recognized him as one of her floor-sleepers from a few years earlier. This time, he was clean and his clothes were those of a clerk of some kind rather than grungy cast-offs.

For his part, there was no surprise in his eyes to see a woman rather than a man. "Good afternoon, Reb," he said. "I wanted to thank you for your help four years ago. Without it, I probably would have died."

"Roses?" she asked.

"For a lovely lady, yes."

Still standing in the doorway, she replied, "How…how did you know? I thought I was careful!"

"May I come in?" he asked.

Feeling embarrassed at her lack of manners, she opened the door wider and stepped aside. He handed her the bouquet, removed his hat, and moved toward the sofa. Never having been given flowers before, Reb was at a loss as to what to do with them. I suggested she put them in a pitcher of water, since she had no vase. This she did while the man glanced around the empty house.

"It looks different without all the people," he commented.

Reb offered him a cup of coffee – she always had a pot going – then invited him to sit.

"My apologies," she said, "but I do not remember your name. And how did you know I was female?"

He laughed. "First things first. I'm not sure I ever told you my name. You were so busy helping everyone else, you really didn't have time for conversation, did you? My name is James Black, but most people call me Jamie.

"As to how I know about you? If one observes, it's not difficult. I caught a glimpse of you going from your bedroom to the bathroom early one morning before you thought anyone was awake. It was easy to see your curves under your bathrobe. Most importantly, though, your aura gives you away."

Her eyes widened. "You can see my aura?"

Jamie laughed again. "You can see auras, too, if you look. Any witch or wizard can."

Reb became uncomfortable – and suspicious. "Why are you here?"

"As I said, I wanted to thank you. Your offer to house and feed me – and others – during that horrible time kept me alive. I swear it. And…now that I have a decent job, I'd like to take you on a date."

This took Reb completely aback. In all her years, no one had asked her out. She liked her independence and wanted no part of the regular path women followed to marriage and children. She had purposely cultivated a detached air so no one, even men who liked men, thought her worth approaching. Jamie, obviously, was different.

After a few moments' thought, Reb declined. "I thank you, but I am not interested in dating or anything it might lead to."

Jamie was not to be deterred. "Well, then. How about two friends going out to dinner? I won't ask for anything more, but I would like to get to know you better. You fascinate me."

To dinner and conversation, Reb agreed. So began a friendship between an Earth witch and an Air wizard. Reb continued to dress as a man when out in public, and Jamie pointedly ignored the looks the couple got. They spent many evenings on her back porch, comparing magical notes or talking politics over glasses of whiskey. When the air was heavy and still, as it frequently was on the Bay, Jamie created a cooling breeze – just enough for the two of them.

Reb was still quite circumspect, though. Jamie knew nothing of how she had first made her money. Now that she was legitimate, though, she had no qualms about showing him how she made jewelry and even made him a signet ring as a birthday gift two years into their association. This he removed from his finger and put on a chain around his neck the day he came by to tell her his number had come up in the draft lottery. He was off to fight for his country in what you call World War II.

Reb once again felt it her duty to help where she could while the men were away. This time, she found a job at a nearby rail yard, helping to refurbish and maintain the cars. Since the cars were made of metal, it was something that came naturally to her, although she *did* learn to weld the same way humans did. She befriended a co-worker, a woman from Denver who had migrated to the area looking for a good job, and within two months, invited Jane to live with her until Jane's husband returned from the front. Jane taught

Reb how to grow and can food, and they transformed Reb's tiny backyard into a lush garden. Luckily, Jane was an Earth witch with an affinity for plants. The hours working at the yard were long, and there was little time left to actually tend the garden after work. Jane's magic helped things grow well even when they were neglected.

Letters arrived sporadically from Jamie and Albert, Jane's husband. They contained little in the way of actual news and occasionally had black splotches on them where the censors had caught sensitive information but mostly, it was about how the men were living rough, the camaraderie in their unit, and how much they missed the women. Reb tried to keep her letters to Jamie light-hearted, telling him of working at the rail yard and her adventures in gardening and canning.

This war and the transformation of women to workers was a good thing for Reb. *Finally,* her choice of clothing no longer set her apart. She threw the tin of pomade away, grew her hair out, stopped binding her breasts, and started acting completely like herself again. It was freeing.

Albert came home two years after he left, missing his right leg from the knee down. He was offered a desk job at a naval base near San Diego. Jane bade a tearful farewell to Reb as she left to join her husband, both women promising to write.

Jamie, however, never came home. Three months before the war was declared over, a package arrived from Jamie's mother. In it was a letter telling Reb he had been killed somewhere in the South Pacific, along with his signet ring on the chain. "He loved you, you know," the letter said. "He knew you would never marry him, but you were his everything. I know you made this for him, and he would want you to have it as a remembrance."

Reb tearfully slipped the chain over her head. It never left her neck again. Nor did she ever date again. In her own way, she had fallen in love with Jamie and did not feel he could be replaced.

When the war was over, the men returned, and the women found themselves without jobs again. Reb was still comfortable in a financial way, but restlessness had set in. Jamie had taught her to drive before leaving for the war, and she decided it would be a good time to see more of the country. She purchased a mobile home, sold the Emeryville cottage, and we hit the road, as you say.

For the next five years, we toured the United States, seeing sights Reb had only read about in books and magazines. From the

Grand Canyon, to the rocky coast of Maine, to the northern Rockies and over to Puget Sound, Reb and I saw all the beauty nature had to offer. But she still felt dissatisfied with her life.

We were sitting on the ground next to a lighthouse overlooking the Pacific Ocean when she realized what she missed was working with metal. She had made no jewelry since before the war started, and once the men took her job at the rail yard back, there was no longer even iron to turn her hand to. And, alarmingly, she missed the thrill of burglary. I tried to talk her into buying precious metals from a reputable source and making the rings and brooches as she once had, but she shook her head.

"That's not as satisfying. I want to hoodwink the rich. It's so much fun to steal things right from under their noses. And because I transform their stuff into something else, I don't have to worry about pawn shops and police."

I thought she was mad. Perhaps she was. Life had become much more civilized in the years since she originally started thieving, and there were more police around. I refrained from pointing out she was considered rich, too.

Then came the Korean War, again sending a lot of young men to fight overseas. We were still in the Pacific Northwest and Reb decided there were a lot of older rich people in Portland...enough to take up her burgling activities again. We were still living in the motor home, and that was too large – and conspicuous – to drive around city streets. We parked in a national park not too far from the city, and Reb purchased a used car to drive to the neighborhoods she scouted. There was one extremely large mansion that caught her eye. Something that large *must* have residents with a lot of jewelry, she decided. But watching the comings and goings taught her otherwise. The residents looked more middle-class than rich, and the women, even in evening attire, wore little jewelry, much less dripped with it as they had just forty years earlier.

She decided on another tack. Newspapers still had gossip columns and reported the comings-and-goings of the upper class. Picking one announced society ball at random, she parked her car across the street from the hotel. We quietly watched everyone who entered and left. There was one older couple who appeared to have the kind of jewelry Reb was looking for. At least, the man's cufflinks were heavy gold; the woman wore a tiara, and her necklace sparkled like a crystal chandelier in the lights of the hotel's *porte cochère*. Reb started her engine while the chauffeur ensured his passengers were comfortable and, waiting for a few cars to get in between, followed them home.

"Home" was a smaller building than the one Reb had originally looked at, but no less ostentatious. We watched as the couple went into the front door and the chauffeur drove the car around the back. An hour later, all lights seemed to be extinguished in the house, and Reb decided to make her move. We stole around to the back of the house where she assumed there was a door to the kitchen and probably servants' stairs. She posted me as a lookout once again, and although I saw no light, my ears heard movement in the garage just a few paces away from the house. I told her what I heard, but she shrugged off my warning, telling me the chauffeur probably slept above where the car was parked and would not be leaving for the rest of the night. Crouching down to get a good look, she found that in the intervening years, locks had changed. She struggled to alter the structure of the lock, which was now steel – something she had not encountered previously. I fed her energy, but even that was not enough for her to quickly discern the different elements of the metal, much less do anything with them. Five minutes passed, then ten. I urged her to give up, but she would not. "I will *not* be defeated!" she told me.

I had only a split second to warn her. The chauffeur came out of the garage, shouted, "Thief!" and fired a pistol. She turned to see what I had warned her about, and I only registered her surprise as the bullet entered her heart before I melted into the ether.

Epilogue

"And that was my life until I met you," Fudge said.

"Wow," I said. "So you were in the ether about fifty years this time? I do wonder about that personality matching thing you told me about.

"And although you lived through what I consider to be historical events and had some interesting experiences, it still sounds like *life*, some good, some bad."

"If you say so," Fudge replied. *"It is what it has been and will be."*

Fudge started giving himself his sixty-fifth bath of the day. He seemed totally unconcerned with the lives and deaths of his previous humans, and while he'd told me a *story*, it was still related in a very factual manner.

"Do you mourn the loss of your humans?" I asked. "You don't seem to."

He paused his bath and gave the cat equivalent of a shrug. *"Life and death are all part of the cycle. It is difficult to feel sad when you know the humans have lived — and died — as they were meant to."*

I considered this. My parents had died when I was seventeen, a lifetime ago it seemed, and I still missed them. A boyfriend had been killed in front of my eyes, and despite the fact I wasn't deeply in love with him, there was a hole in the place he'd occupied in my life. Thinking about losing my friends Cassandra, Louise or hell, even Ev, my ogre boss, my heart hitched. I found it almost impossible to be as pragmatic as my familiar about the life-and-death cycle.

"Okay," I persisted. "Let's put it another way. Was your life enriched by your association with your humans? Would something in you be missing if you hadn't been with them?"

"Of course!" My cat was indignant. *"My experiences with them added to my knowledge. Each contributed their unique way of doing things. As have you. As will my humans after you."*

I wasn't going to get my cat to admit he had feelings. But I knew he did. It was evident in bed every night when he nested in my hair, curled up next to my back and purred. It was just a matter of time before I could get him to own up to it. I could wait. I picked him up and hugged him. I wouldn't want to lose him, either.

Fudge snuggled back, purred for a moment, then struggled in my arms and hopped down. *"Now I have told my tale, I am hungry. Is there any tuna?"*

Acknowledgements

Every book takes a village – even (especially?) ones that are indie-published. My profound thanks to everyone who encouraged me to write Fudge's story – it was a blast to research and write.

Thanks also to the many historians who wrote about the times Fudge lived through. I lost count of the books, magazine articles, and web pages I read to make it as historically-authentic as possible while still maintaining the magic. Naturally, the spirit currently known as Fudge and his various humans did not exist, but there are a lot of historical figures in this book; many were quite interesting characters in their own right.

Laura Perry, editor extraordinaire, did her usual bang-up job of correcting my faux pas. I couldn't do it without her.

Fiona Jayde, the designer of the awesome cover, always lends her brilliance. Since I can't draw a straight line with a ruler, her creative efforts are much appreciated.

Finally, to my husband Pete. His constant encouragement is what keeps me going.

About the Author

A semi-retired accountant, Master Herbalist, author and witch, Deborah J. "DJ" Martin is the author of non-fiction books about herbs as well as this fiction series.

She abandoned frozen Minnesota many moons ago and now lives in the woods of the southern Appalachian Mountains with her husband, four cats, and numerous woodland creatures. If you can't find DJ in the garden or visiting her grandchildren, check Facebook http://www.facebook.com/authordjmartin,Twitter @authordjmartin, or her website http://www.authordjmartin.com.

A personal note to the reader:

If you enjoyed this book, would you take a few seconds to let your friends know about it? Word of mouth is the best way for an author to build an audience and I'd really appreciate the help. Thanks!